I WAS AN OP DEMON LORD BEFORE I GOT ISEKAI'D TO THIS BORING CORPORATE JOB!!!!!!!!!!!!!!!

I WAS AN OP DEMON LORD BEFORE I GOT ISEKAI'D TO THIS BORING CORPORATE JOB!!!!!!!!!!!!!!

EPISODE 1: EVERYBODY WANTS TO CALL ME "MASTER!"

REGINA WATTS

PAINTED BLIND
PUBLISHING
LITERARY ALCHEMY

PAINTED BLIND
PUBLISHING
LITERARY ALCHEMY

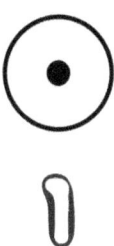

THE NEW SECRETARY stares at me every time I get up for a smoke break. I assumed earlier she was into me, but the third time I pass her desk it's just so brazen that I think for sure she's judging my habits. Probably one of those stuck-up types who like to jog at the ass-crack of dawn.

Me? I can barely get up with the alarm. Especially when it's my fate to drag myself to this place day after day.

This new Beatrix chick, though, with her flowing blonde hair and piercing blue eyes...she could make it a little easier coming into work every day. Her blouse shows such a dangerous amount of cleavage that I'm amazed management hasn't said something. Who'd want to, though? Don't want to restrict her self-expression.

Maybe I'll introduce myself. Figure out if she's into me. And if she's not, I'll convince her that she is.

I put out the cigarette and head back inside Helcom's main office building. Barely seeing the gray carpeted hall back to the cubicles where I'm stuffed away all day, I focus on one thing and one thing only: Beatrix's desk.

There she is, peering over its round edge, already piercing me with eyes like daggers.

Before I make it anywhere near her, my boss steps out of his office. Gabe is a tall, wide guy with a friendly smile and no discernible personality besides being a tool of the corporation…and a tool in general. He lifts his eyebrows as though he's surprised to bump into me, though I know he timed this moment.

"Vic! There you are. Do you have a minute?"

Turning my gritted teeth into a smile that could drop him dead for as dark as it is, I straighten up and force myself to say, "Of course."

"It's only a few minutes…"

Still with a smile as perfect as a Ken doll, Gabe steps aside and shuts the door behind me. "How are you, Vic? Coming to the department pool tournament on Friday?"

"I'll have to see what my schedule's like…my mother's been trying to get me on the phone all day."

"You're a good son," says the manager approvingly, nodding as he sinks into his seat. "If you would pay as much mind to the company, I wouldn't have to talk to you right now."

My blood runs cold with insult. Somehow, I contain my fury. Leaning forward in his seat with his hands folded on the edge of the desk, Gabe says firmly. "Let's get down to brass tacks. I can see your productivity is way down. Projects are taking you longer. You're coming in late from lunch all the time, calling in once a week. Listen: I get it. I mean, you're young! You've got a life. There's plenty of things most of us would rather be doing than working in here, let me tell you."

Like burning your eyes out with cigarettes, Gabriel. I realize I'm grinding my teeth when he pauses his patter as though awaiting a response.

"Uh-huh," I supply.

"But we've all been there, or will be there. When an employee is there, well…if nothing changes, they don't tend to stay *here.*"

"I'll try to shape up."

"It's just as much my fault as it is yours," says my boss, waving his hands with a smile and taking that casual tone that I hate. "Between you and me, this place is a snoozefest! Engineering is such a solitary department. I have a lot more fun when I'm managing people." Looking thoughtful, he wags a finger at me, squints, then snatches up his pen to make a note to himself. "Maybe I'll talk to Raphael about openings in sales."

"*Sales?*" I scoff. The last thing I want to do is interact with clients. "I like where I'm at. Besides, I don't have any background in selling."

"Always good to learn," says Gabe brightly. All smiles, he looks up at me and lifts his blond eyebrows. "Heck, Vic! You might find you love it once you've tried it."

"Maybe. So…is that all?"

"I don't want to drag this on and on, so let's just table all this and assume the problem will have fixed itself by the time of your formal review in June. I just wanted to give you a friendly warning, rather than a formal one."

With a wink and a grin, Gabriel swings around to his computer and tells me, no longer looking my way, "See you Friday, I hope!"

"Hope so…"

In the hall, I'm more annoyed to find Beatrix has vacated her desk than I am with the previous conversation. Gabe is right: I've been in a fugue state. Frankly, I'm barely able to remember what I did this last weekend. Monday is almost over, yet a whole week still stares me down…ugh. Sighing, scratching my head, I fix my dark hair back into place and make my way around the corner of my cubicle.

Beatrix, the gray skirt of her suit riding high up her thick thighs, leans back against my desk and locks eyes with me as I stop short.

"Uh—"

"Come out with me tonight," she says, her hand lifting to the top button of her blouse and slipping it free. The lace of a red bra peeks from beneath the fabric, cherry bright against the pale milk of her skin. I inhale sharply, looking up into her face for a hint of insanity.

Instead, I see deadly seriousness.

"Uh, well, I—"

"Your name is Victor Legion, isn't it?"

I swallow, nodding.

"Please…Victor."

Biting her lip, the new girl leans forward from her perch and crosses the few feet between us to lean against me. Her hand fits to my heart as she gazes up into my face, my nostrils filling with the scent of rosewater and—charcoal?

"Please," she whispers to me again. "I need to talk to you. In private."

What the hell could this lady possibly want? Astonished, I try to think of what the problem could be, but ultimately the statuesque aesthetics of her face and body win out. "All right," I tell her. "You want to meet for a drink or two somewhere?"

We settle on a place, Frank's Bar—practically across the street from the Helcom campus—and, looking relieved I've agreed, Beatrix slides past me out of the cube. "Don't back out on me," she urges. "I need to talk to you, Legion."

"You lucky dog," whispers my neighbor as her heels tap out of earshot. Laughing, I lean around his cubicle and wiggle my eyebrows.

"Isn't there a difference between luck and skill?"

Mike shakes his head, his desk chair swiveling to face me. "Skill is what men like *me* have to develop...luck is what men looking like you have to work with."

"If you'd just get some contacts and reduce the number of action figures," I say with a brisk glance over the decorations of his desk, "you'd probably have an easier time."

"No woman worth loving won't also love my collectibles. Gabe was looking for you."

I sigh, slapping the edge of Mike's cube. "I know. I don't even want to get into it right now...in fact, I'm thinking about getting *out*."

"You think it's really a good idea to duck out after the manager's got you looking so hangdog?"

"What better time? He's already thinking about his low expectations of me...we'll start fresh tomorrow. Cover for me if somebody asks, will you?"

With an indulgent shake of his head, my friend exchanges a fist-bump with me before turning back to his work. "I'll try not to worry about you, Vic."

"Why worry? Things will work out, or they won't. Either way, I'm going to choose to do what makes me happy."

And right now, getting out of work makes me happy. With Gabe's office door shut, I sneak right past, Beatrix's sharp eyes on me the whole while. She's a weird chick, but, well, weird chicks tend to be fun for a little while. Besides, secretary is a cursed position at this department. They tend to leave after a few months…and not always because I've stopped returning their calls.

After a short drive home to clean up before my impromptu date, I sigh, loosen my tie, and check my voicemails while standing in the living room of my small condo. One from a telemarketer allegedly wanting to talk about my ancient Lincoln's non-existent extended warranty, and one from my mother.

"Victor? Sweetheart, it's your mother. Call me back when you get this, please! I've been trying to call you all day."

"And I've been trying to work all day," I mutter to the phone, making a mental note to eventually fulfill her request but for now staying focused on showering, changing into a fresh set of clothes, and making sure the apartment doesn't look like a total sty in case somebody ends up coming home with me. I leave out a *Forbes* on the coffee table to look like a serious young professional, and I even stop to make my bed. It's the little details that make all the difference in a seduction.

Not that Beatrix seems like a hard case. I've never seen a woman like her—let alone one who's so forward. My blood heats to think of her perched on the edge of my desk. After checking myself in the mirror to fix the collar of my shirt, I hurry back out the door to make to the bar.

Melody, my neighbor across the hall, stands in her own doorway with one hand on the knob and the other raised in surprise.

"Oh, Vic!"

Damn! Usually, running into Melody is a thrill of its own. She's a gentle, quiet woman with beautiful cascades of silvery lilac hair that, the one or two times we've ridden the elevator together, overwhelms my senses with the phantoms of flowers and incense. I've been warming her up slowly since she's so shy, but to my absolute shock she smiles at me today. "I was just coming to ask you if you'd like to join me for dinner tonight!"

"Ah!" I laugh apologetically, pressing my hands together and bowing slightly to her. "I really hate to disappoint you, but I actually have a"—I almost call it a 'date' but decide at the last second to switch to—"work thing tonight, and I really have to go."

Her gentle face falls, and even I'm consumed by guilt to see it. "Oh, really? Gosh—"

"I'm really sorry."

"No—no, it's fine. I should have asked sooner! Um… sorry—have fun—"

"Melody—"

But her door is already shut. I curse myself, shaking my head, and make my brisk way to the elevator. I like to think I have a way with women, but Melody is a tough case. One of these days, though…or, more likely, one of these nights.

This night, though, I walk into Frank's Bar.

Beatrix is already sitting in a booth in the dark back corner, out of earshot of the few people shooting pool.

"Thank you for coming, sir," she says, standing and embracing me when I'm close enough for her to grasp. Those hypnotically large tits of hers press against my chest and I clear my throat, patting her on the back.

"My pleasure, uh, Beatrix…but you can call me—"

"I took the liberty of getting you your favorite drink," she says, pushing a vodka tonic over to me as I sit.

My eyes whip back and forth between her and the glass. "How did you know that?"

"You must promise to stay in the booth while I tell you."

A little late for that. Between her weird fixation with me throughout the day, her forward demand that I come meet her, and now this drink order, I can't help but feel something weird is going on. Scoffing, I look around for the hidden camera and ask her in as low a voice as I can manage, "What are you? Some kind of stalker?"

"I am one of your four most faithful slaves," she responds, looking me right in the eye, "and you, Legion, are a demon lord with powers so great that the very angels fear your name."

I HESITATE, MY mind struggling to parse this claim.

The words settle in.

I laugh.

Beatrix says nothing, her hands folded before her as Gabe's had been only earlier today.

"A *demon* lord, huh? Sister, I think you forgot your medication."

"I'm not joking, sir."

"And neither am I." Forcing myself to stop laughing, reminding myself that I'm dealing with a mentally ill person here, I look at her more seriously. "I don't know if this is some sort of joke, or what, but you just started at

Helcom today. When you say something like that to me and I know nothing else about you, what am I supposed to think but that you're crazy?"

"I can prove it to you," she says, completely unperturbed by my statements. "The fact that you have not left the booth means you are at least interested in what I have to say, so let me build a case before you reject it out-of-hand."

"I haven't left the booth because you asked me nicely not to…but, go on." Settling back in my seat, arms folded over my chest, I stare her down and tell her, "Prove away."

"What do you remember about this weekend?"

I scoff.

Then, like an animal frozen at the approach of the car, my body goes rigid.

What *do* I remember about this weekend?

"This last weekend," I clarify to buy myself a few seconds of time.

"Yes, sir. What do you remember about the past two days?"

"I…"

My lips press thin.

Beatrix waits.

After a long time, she says: "What about the past month? Do you remember any of that? What movies you have seen, what you have eaten? What did you dream last night? Do you have any evidence at all that you have even been conscious for your entire life, aside from a handful of memories that exist to give your life a context?"

Though I open my mouth, no sound emits. It closes again and my brow furrows. Staring off somewhere beside Beatrix, my mind races rapidly through the implications of this great, vast gap standing just behind me.

In my pocket, my phone buzzes.

Distracted from my thoughts, I reach for it on automatic to see who it is and silence it. Beatrix reaches across the table and snatches my wrist.

"Don't look at it," she urges me. "It wants to distract you."

"What wants to distract me, and from what?"

"The simulation. It wants to distract you from the truth."

Though I shake my head, I do lower my hand again. "What is this, *The Matrix?*"

She looks at me in confusion, like she's never heard of the movie before. These crazy hipsters…pretending they haven't seen popular movies, trying to trick people into thinking they're demon lords.

"The system the conspirators established is dedicated to preventing you from discerning the truth at any cost." Beatrix resumes without missing too many beats, her tone still laden with urgency. "How many inconveniences have you encountered today? Inconveniences you have had to overcome to find yourself here with me?"

I catch myself thinking about it even though I shouldn't be absorbing a word this crazy woman says. But, at the same time…my boss, my mother, my neighbor. Are these just coincidences? Of course they are. Why am I even asking myself that question?

"Okay," I tell her, neglecting my drink in case she's slipped something in it while waiting for me, "if I'm this person who you say I am, why am I here? Why am I just some shmuck working at an office job if I have all of this power?"

"Because we are at war, Master," she says a little too loudly for my liking. I glance around, glad most other patrons there are involved in their own conversations. Only Frank can hear, and letting him overhear is cheaper and faster than repeating all this to a therapist.

Still…this place is close to work, and I don't want the conversation getting overheard by the wrong pair of ears.

Clearing my throat, I slide out of my side of the booth and into hers. "Keep your voice down, okay?" I struggle to moderate the volume of my own, keeping my hands folded upon the tabletop in case she or an onlooker have the wrong idea.

But it sort of seems like Beatrix has the wrong idea anyway. Our knees touch beneath the table and her cheeks turn vibrant scarlet, her eyes glazing over and her pouting lips parting in a sensuous, barely stifled gasp.

Ah, man…my dick gets hard in a second.

"How generous you are to sit so close to me, sir," she whispers urgently, pressing against me with her blue eyes lifted toward my face. "Oh, Master—I shouldn't touch you! I can't think when I do."

Shuddering, the insane(ly hot) woman peels herself away from me and presses back against the wall of the establishment. Still radiating desire, she fixes the collar of her blouse and keeps her hand there, unconsciously tugging it open just a bit as she speaks to me.

"There is an age-old war," she says, now more softly. I relax, trying to get my mind under control while letting her get her…whatever this is…out of her system. "I won't bore you with the details because you know them all too well. All humanoid beings do, for it is passed in the backgrounds of all artworks and the enforced morals of mankind. But now hear this, sire: That you, my Master, are a King among Princes. The most powerful, most worthy of demons in this or any other dimension—and the leader in our war against celestial realms."

"No kidding," I say, trying to sound interested.

"You don't believe me."

"No, I mean, well—it's all just a little much."

"That is because you have been thrust down into a world where it *is* a little much. The angels are brainwashing you."

The sentence makes my scalp tingle in a weird, unpleasant way that I really don't like. Sounds like some cult shit. No thanks. "Look, Beatrix—"

She forces herself to grab me around the forearm and, as she does, whimpers with erotic ecstasy. I grit my teeth and try to keep myself calm.

"You are bound in this prison of flesh by seven planetary seals," says the crazy secretary, her voice breathless and her eyes hooded with desire. "I can tell you more, but—"

"No, thanks."

Shaking myself out of her grip—wrenching, really, and finding myself shocked at her strength when her hand seems so soft and delicate—I pull out my wallet and toss down a ten. "That's for the drink, and for Frank's trouble. Whatever you're buying, I'm not selling."

"Something is going to happen to you tonight," says Beatrix before I'm more than two steps away from the booth.

"What's going to happen?"

"The prison will sense the inklings of an escape attempt and come looking to rectify the problem."

I shake my head. "Sorry," I tell her, "I just can't take anymore."

Embarrassed for Beatrix—and for myself, for wasting time with her—I nod to Frank, haul ass through the restaurant, and hit the warm night air with my cigarettes already in-hand. I take a drag, struggle to peer through the city lights to see if any stars of interest are hanging around in the sky (a little early yet) and decide to take the highway back to my apartment.

Tucson is not a convenient town to get around in. The highway is awkwardly formatted and really only useful if you're going north to south or vice versa. Sometimes, though, it's good to take it just to speed a little and clear my head.

I listened to that crazy chick too long. Why? Because she was hot, of course. But…well, that isn't all.

It's an absurd idea she proposed. At the same time, it's so alluring. Who doesn't want to be more than just some guy at a desk?

Then, well…she was pretty revved up at my mere touch. Maybe this is some sexual roleplaying thing? I churn the possibilities wildly through my head and, distracted, fiddle with my radio with one hand while keeping the cigarette pinched between my fingers on the wheel. By the time I look up, the black Benz careening behind me is much too close for comfort.

I wait for them to change lanes, but they don't.

The car roars closer and closer to mine. Agitated, I change lanes for them to let them have all the road they want.

They follow.

Lips pursed, my brain tingling with emergency signals, I flick my cigarette out the window, roll it up, and turn down the radio.

When I hit the gas, the person riding my tail hits the gas. When I ease up, they drop back a length or two to keep from rear-ending me.

At first.

It's as we start to pass the old airplane cemetery—and I realize how far I've driven along the highway with this person on my fender—that the expensive car leaps forward and bumps into mine. My age-old Lincoln is not what it used to be, and the car produces an unpleasant grind. I swear and slam the gas, not sure what this person's problem is and not really interested in finding out.

The next slam is harder, and while I'm still recovering from the shock of it their car continues grinding into mine for a long five seconds. Teeth clenched, I check the road around, throw the car over one lane and slam the brakes.

My pursuer shoots past me.

Hating every second of what I have to do, I tell my wonderful car, "I'm sorry," pat her dash, then flip a nasty u-turn over a median which, while flat and free of fences, is also absolutely covered in desert plants of all kinds of sharp, tangling, engine-obliterating variety. I remind myself to make an appointment with the mechanic while mounting the northbound highway and earning a loud, well-justified spate of honks from passerby.

In my rear-view, the Benz emulates my u-turn.

Palms sweating, I floor it.

With more people trying to get to downtown to party or eat at the end of a workday, the traffic is a fair bit heavier. Helpful in some ways, more dangerous in others. I weave between cars to keep as much distance as possible between myself and my pursuer, but they are dogged. Between the stunts they were pulling and the tint of their windows I wasn't able to get a good look at their face, but their license plate ended in 368, and I chant it to myself like a useless mantra while focusing on getting—where?

Off the highway, for a start. But when I take the next exit, I'm just around the corner when the Benz appears in the rear view, merging over to pursue me. Trying to stay calm and focused, I decide to loop back around to the highway and shake them off with the help of a particularly confusing intersection.

But on my way back around, along a trail leading beneath an overpass, my eye is caught by, of all things, a woman. For a second she seems like a statue, but since I drive past this place all the time and have never seen anything perched upon the edge of the overpass, I take a second look. Her beautiful dark hair flaps in the breeze like her coat, and though I catch only a glimpse of her, her athletic body and stern demeanor glue her image in my mind.

Especially with the rifle in her hands.

I almost ask myself aloud what that was, but I don't have to waste the rhetorical breath. Somehow, strangely, I know what she's there for, even if I don't know how I know…or, for that matter, how she does. Yet, all the same, as I blaze beyond the overpass and roll down my window, I listen. My car slows to a more relaxed, legal pace.

Above the sound of the whipping highway and all its busy traffic, I swear I discern the crack of a sniper's rifle.

I don't see the Benz again on the way home, though I'd might as well find it around every corner I turn. Hands numb, I nix plans to get back on the highway. Instead I take the city streets the long, slow way home.

Part of me wants to get back as fast as possible, but the rest of me knows it doesn't matter. The car needs a break after what it's been through, and so do I. Every light in the city can be red for all we care. Amazed at the pounding of my heart, I stop off to buy a six-pack of beer before finding my way to my condo in a daze.

And when the door swings open at the touch of my key, I find my living room has been swallowed by another dimension.

TO BE FAIR, I don't know right away that I am standing in another dimension. Open-mouthed, the beers still cradled in my arm like a precious infant, I look round what should be my carefully furnished living room to find…nothing. Darkness. The essence of space and time, or the womb in which both are born.

Who cares? The important thing is that I do *not* find my apartment.

"What the fuck is going *on* tonight?"

"I told you, Master."

Vertiginous without my sense of direction, I whip around in the sound of the voice. My front door has vanished, too. Wherever this place is, I'm stuck here… but I'm stuck here with Beatrix, who looks unlike any woman I've ever seen.

In fact, I would say she looks like a demon.

The business suit has disappeared, but the crimson bustier I had taken for a bra remains pushing up those great globes that would catch my eye were it not for the four horns projecting from her wild golden mane. The nails once more professionally manicured earlier today are firetruck red, and they shine almost as bloody bright as her now matching eyes. I would focus on them longer if I could, but a white hint of tight stomach between her bustier and her panties keeps luring my eye toward her fishnet stockings, her bright red heels, her lashing demon tail. It takes me a few seconds to realize she has wings, too, although they appear to be made of flame. Are they wings at all, or only something I perceive as wings?

"I told you I was telling the truth."

"What did you do to my apartment?"

Pouting, toying girlishly with a lock of blonde hair, Beatrix says, "I didn't do anything, Master. I know I shouldn't come to your nest without permission, but it's an emergency circumstance. You need to be woken up."

Kneeling before me, her face once more flushed to have my eyes upon her, the demoness gazes up at me and whispers, "We are here to do that. The apartment is gone for now because you are beginning to see the truth. As you remember, it remembers."

It's all so impossible to believe. So incredible to believe. How could any of this be true? But—looking around to find myself with a void instead of an apartment, and then studying the demon girl kneeling in front of me, I consider one of two possibilities. I've died, and my version of heaven is really weird…or she's right, and this is true.

Either way, it's starting to seem like these crazy ideas might have a very real-world impact on my life.

The dark-haired woman on the overpass flashes through my mind and I study Beatrix closely, somehow remembering one of her pieces of what I had assumed to be nonsense.

"'We.' The other three of the four?"

"Yes," she whispers, crawling toward me on her hands and knees in a way I have to admit I admire. "Yes, Master, your loyal choir of attendants…we won't let anyone take you from us, sir."

As she reaches my shoe, she rolls over upon some unnerving invisible floor. Flat on her back, her legs lightly splayed, she clasps her hands over her heart and smiles dreamily up at me. "These wicked angels think they can seal you away, but we'll help you win your power back, and your memory, and your position in Hell."

"Will you help me get my condo back, please?"

Laughing softly, the demoness gazes up at me and says, "Only you can do that, sir…it is one of your gifts, and one of the first seals to break. The seal of Sol: Manifestation."

"And how do I break these seals, exactly?"

Beatrix smiles, a hint of fang shining from behind her pink lip. "By overcoming the challenge of the seal-holder, or by convincing them to destroy the seal they protect. Only Sol is different: born from simple self-awareness. From the realization of your true nature."

"But why did it all disappear in the first place?"

"Because you are beginning to wake up. The prison is destabilizing."

"So you're to thanks for all my trouble, huh?" Lifting my foot, I press the edge of my shoe to her cheek. Delighted, eyelids fluttering, the demoness moans. I dig the leather in a little and throb at the sight of her ecstasy. "Is it a bad pun to observe how horny you are?"

"Oh, sir…all demons are horny, but especially for you…yes, oh! Your cruelest backhanded slap leaves me wet for days!"

Damn. Clearing my throat, glancing around as I had at the bar, I set down the beers and kneel beside the demoness at my feet. The wing-like aura of hers has settled down into a bed of flame almost indiscernible from her golden hair, both spread beneath her in a welcoming cushion that I find gives no heat and does not burn—at least, does not burn me.

"You like it rough, don't you?"

"Yes, Master, oh—"

My hand fills itself with Beatrix's cheek and jaw. Amazing! How is this woman real? How does she feel so warm, so physical? It seems like I should be dreaming. I caress down her neck while looking into her eyes. "You and these other three, this choir, my devoted servants… is there anything you will not do for me?"

"Nothing." Her red eyes sparkle in the void. Moaning while my hand cups her breast through the scarlet lace of her bustier, the demoness moans like a bitch in heat. "No, Master! We are slaves to your will, your creations to do with as pleases you…oh, Master, yes—"

Her nipple, already stiff, reaches an aching peak beneath my teasing. I lower my head and kiss her panting mouth, eliciting a moan from her that's so high and sharp I might as well have slid a hand into her panties. "Master! Thank you, oh, yes, please, no demon could touch me like you do! My body was made for your hand…oh, sir…"

With her legs spread so welcomingly, I give into temptation and slide my hand down into the front of her little black panties. She gasps, gazing up at me with an almost scandalized moan while I slowly tease the hairless mound within. Beatrix really is soaking wet for me, which seems almost impossible…but then again, my dick is stiff in my pants without her doing much more than lay at my feet, so who am I to judge?

Soon, as my fingertip trails down the cleft of her vulva and tickles her clit while she gasps and moans, Beatrix unzips my trousers and draws me into the open. I barely even realize how much I'm suffering until her hand, soft as silk, strokes along my length as though petting a dog. While I strain in her caress, she moans and spreads her legs all the more to me.

"Let me be your toy," begs the demoness, her pussy on ready display when I draw aside her panties to admire the sight of her. While I groan at the sight of her drenched petals, I slowly arch my hips into the steady work of her hand. Her neck contorts along with her body and soon her damp lips brush the throbbing head of my dick, her long tongue trailing out to wiggle back and forth, then all around it.

"Fill me with your noble seed, Master," she murmurs, each word another vibration of lust through my length, "and begin to recall your true self."

When I sink a finger into the flooded channel between her arousal-pink labia, I can't resist a second longer. Have I ever felt a woman so wet in all my life? Have I ever lived a life before today? I'm not sure, and I don't care. I push down my pants and slide aside her panties, and while the demoness groans at the urgency, I support her hips and plunge my bare cock into her.

Together, we cry out. The first stab radiates through us both like a shock, a great shared tremor. Then, while her eyes flutter and fix on mine, I pound into her again. Again. Her cunt squeezes viselike around me, overflowing with pleasure that encourages me to be rough. "Yes," she says amid gasps, her voice so loud and desperate that I think it's a good thing my apartment has been replaced by this void, "yes, yes, fuck! Oh, Master, this is just what I've needed!"

"Glad you like it rough…I like a girl who can take a good, hard fucking."

"Yes, yes, oh, yes, Master! Keep going, oh, yes, please,

mark your obedient little slave with your unholy cum. Let me overflow in it! Baptize me in it! Master, Master!"

Every stroke into her resonates through my body to the very tips of my fingers. I bury them in her hair to kiss her and, while my tongue tangles with hers, my hand bumps those hard horns of hers. She gasps at the contact and shudders as violently as she did in the booth—maybe more.

Grinning, I lift my head and gaze into her eyes. "You like it when I touch your horns, do you?"

"O-oh, sir!" Her moan becomes a high keen of ecstasy as I caress the lengths of the curved pair of horns upon her head. Soon she's almost screaming, her hips arching up to meet my thrusts with vigor second to none. "Mm! Mm, yes, please, yes, touch me there—oh, oh, my horns are so sensitive, I love it when you pet my horns…oh, it's almost as nice as when you touch my pussy, as when you fuck me, fuck, fuck, fuck!"

Her scream reaches a new height and her hips slam up against mine. I gasp, watching with true appreciation as her body contorts and her fluttering pussy squeezes the life out of me. While I thrust into her pulses, her long tongue lolls out and her tail thrashes upon the invisible floor. "Hn! Sir! Sir…oh…"

Whimpering, moaning, writhing, Beatrix arches her back and swiftly unclasps the hooks of her bustier. Letting the pink-tipped globes of her swollen breasts fall from the lace, she throws it all away and wraps her legs around me. Soon, pushing herself up and urging me down, the demoness rides my cock while I enjoy the show and run my hands back over her luscious rear.

"Master, Master! Fuck, I want your cock for eternity… oh, mm, but we have to practice manifesting…oh, let's try it, let's try it now…when you're in this space, manifesting is as easy as visualization. What do you need, Master?"

"A bed," I grunt, barely able to form the words as I strain up against her, always aiming to get just that much deeper into her tight embrace. "Ah—a bed to fuck you in."

"Oh, oh! Oh—then picture it!"

"Now?"

"Now is the best time," she says, gasping as she impales herself upon me at an even faster pace. "Sexual energy is key to all your powers, and mine! Together, we generate the capacity for so much…"

I groan, my whole body wired with the centralized pleasure brought on by this demoness fucking herself on my cock. While she reaches back to support herself against my thigh and give me an even better view of her bouncing breasts, of the white plane of her stomach, of the hint of pussy I see peering from her still merely pushed aside panties, I struggle desperately to think of a bed. A bed! What kind of bed? I don't know. The only thing I can think of is one of those kitschy bachelor beds, a big round thing with purple sheets and room for six or seven, and—

"Look down, Master!"

Drawn from my haze by her moaning voice, I look down at the bed now squeaking along beneath us. I somehow manage a laugh, though it's short and quick. "Hah, look at that—ah, fuck, ah, Beatrix—"

"Call me by my real name here, Master…oh, 'Baphomet,' sir, please!"

"Fine, Baphomet, ah…"

I grit my teeth and sit up a little, kissing and sucking her nipples while she quakes with ecstasy in my lap. While one hand lifts to fondle her horns, the other fits to her backside to squeeze and spread those glorious cheeks. The tip of my finger trails around the pucker of her asshole and I roughly brush my mouth across hers. "I'll bet you like it in every hole, huh, Baphomet?"

"Oh, yes, yes, yes, fuck, I'm a real slut for you, sir! Mn! Yes, your naughty, nasty little whore! O-oh, oh, we all are, we're all such dirty, horny girls!"

"When will we get to meet the others?"

My question falls on deaf ears. As I tease her ass, the stimulation is just too much. Baphomet cries out, her eyes wild and her entire body shuddering with violent passion. She screams for me and I thrust up into her a few more hard times, but the feeling of her sphincter fluttering against my fingertip in sync with her cunt around my dick is just too much to resist.

"You want my cum, do you?"

She gasps, wild-eyed and nodding, begging, "Yes, oh, yes, Master! Daddy! Fill me up, please, please, sir!"

I could get used to the sound of all of that. Gritting my teeth, I grab her by one horn and draw her gasping mouth to mine. While she moans, I stab up into her tight embrace until, at last, the pressure reaches its breaking point and I groan against her tongue. My cock, teased all day by the mere sight of her behind the desk, shoots more than its share of semen deep in her eager pussy. As she trembles, moaning, her eyes rolling with bliss, I hold her close to me and gasp through the waves of pleasure.

With a noise like a moan—or maybe closer to a purr—the demoness gingerly eases herself from off of me with a soft gasp, a little pout, and a gentle caress of my sensitive prick. As it twitches in her hand, she smiles and croons, "I get the feeling you'll wake back up soon…"

"I get that feeling, too." But for now, in the post-orgasm clarity, I become more aware of the luxurious sheets of the bed beneath my body—the comfort of the mattress, too. All of it better quality than anything I had before. "So I can manifest anything with this, huh?"

"Only when you're in your nest, Master...for now. Eventually, you will regain the power to manifest objects in the outside world."

"My nest? Is that what demons call this place?"

"Yes, sire. This is your home, your pocket dimension. Because you were hypnotized by the prison system you forgot its true nature, and it therefore conformed to your hypnotized mind's mundane expectations of it. Since you are breaking the first seal, it is also remembering what it is. You may now alter the contents of your apartment as you see fit, and manifest whatever item you wish."

"An atomic bomb?"

"Is that what you wish?"

"No, too much trouble...just seeing. Uh...a million dollars in cash?"

"Yes, but there will naturally be discrepancies with the serial numbers of the bills."

"Uh-huh, standard monkey's paw dilemma."

"Just so. It is far safer to focus on manifesting your own space for now."

I nod, though I can't help but think of all the things a person can do with a power like this. Can I manifest living things, too? I guess so, if I created the choir like she said I did.

Amazing how quickly demonstration can make a man a believer.

While Baphomet settles herself in my arm, I stare at the ceiling that is there because I expect it to be there. A ceiling implies walls, and when I look down there's those, too—only the walls and ceiling are dark red and rich gold hues instead of the boring white required by the condo association. The light fixtures must be something I've seen in a movie or a magazine at some point, because they are ornate and beautiful pieces of brasswork that certainly didn't come from my imagination alone. Drapes soften the windows now, and the books that line the shelves are more extensive in number than before. Who knows what titles my mind picked for me…I'll have to check later.

"You always have known how to feather a love-nest," Baphomet praises me, her smile dreamy and crooked while she observes our new surroundings. "And the rest?"

"It'll be there when I open the door…I can see it all. The hall, the guest room, the kitchen, the new living room…there's no accounting for space, right? I mean, the nest is an inter-dimensional space of some kind?"

"That's exactly right." With an appropriately devilish grin and a little flick of her pointed tail, Baphomet sits up and stretches. "It can be as big or as small as you like, no matter what the rest of the apartments in this place are like…but you have to be careful, of course, when you're letting humies visit."

"Humies?"

"You really *are* lost in this human identity of yours, huh, sir? 'Humies.' You know! Human normies. They make up most of this prison system you're in…but you have to be careful, sir."

Her demeanor grows stern. She studies me gravely enough that I feel a bit drawn from my post-coital buzz. "There are many out in the world who would like to see your human vessel killed, in which case you will also be annihilated. A great many angels walk the world in the guise of humans—and so do traitorous demons, upstarts who are disloyal to you in their heart of hearts. You must be careful whom you trust."

"I will. But what about you?"

"What about me?"

"How will I contact you if I need you?"

"Oh…well…" Smiling in a sly way, her fingertips trailing over my chest, she said, "Perhaps it's very forward to suggest such a thing as this, but you must remember… before, in your palace, all five of us lived and enjoyed one another in extremely close quarters. My apartment was right next to your suite, Master."

My hand finding the curve of her waist and petting down over her hip, I chuckle. "Are you saying you want to move in with me?"

Normally it would be insane to agree to a thing like that, but, well…this whole day has been pretty insane. Not to mention, after my experience on the road, the idea of having a demoness around the apartment is fairly comforting. If I am who she says I am, then I must have some sort of power locked inside of me somewhere—but until I can access it fully, I may have to lean on friends for help.

Besides…who can resist the thought of having a woman like this around the house?

"All right," I tell her, pulling down her black thong while she moans in anticipation, "sure…you'll have a new room, right beside mine."

She gasps with pleasure at the thought, offering herself as a feast to my eyes while I gaze at what lies beneath her panties. "Yes, please, Master! Please…oh, yes, come use me every night! Wake me from the dead of sleep and satisfy yourself with me. Mn! Oh! Oh, yes, please, Master!"

Finger tickling between those pretty labia of hers, I tear my eyes from the scene only to study her face. "Now, Baphomet," I tell her, smiling, "it sounds like you of all demons should know to be careful what you wish for…"

MY FIRST THOUGHT when the alarm goes off the next morning is that I'd had a nice dream, though I could have done without the whole highway chase scene.

My next thought is that I'd better be careful of the horns of the woman sleeping beside me.

I bolt upright, mouth open in shock.

"You," I say, realizing the bed beneath me is the one from the dream. "You, this—"

"Good morning, Master." With a long, languid stretch that goes from finger to toe to tail, Baphomet rolls upon her side to smile at me from those twinkling crimson eyes. "I pray you're not too tired after last night?"

"Uh—I—uh—no, but—"

"Good…" Sitting upright now, her wonderful breasts catching my eye like magnets snatching up metal files,

Baphomet slides both hands over my chest and pouts through a few errant locks of blonde hair. "You look surprised. Did you change your mind about letting me stay with you?"

"Uh—uh, no, uh—"

"That's good. Oh! Master…" One of her hands has slithered down my stomach to caress the morning wood that's even harder than usual, for reasons which I would think are pretty evident. While I inhale into the sparks of her touch, she blushes and quivers with delight. "You're so extra-hard for me this morning, sir…may I suck your cock?"

Fuck! Like that's even a question. Without even a glance at the clock, seeing that her head is already lowering over me, I tell her, "Oh, sure, sure, please do… ah—"

That uncanny tongue of hers slithers out to tease around my head, lapping lightly at my flesh before relaxing to permit her lips to swallow me into a cavern of delight. While her head bobs down over me and her throat relaxes to take in every inch, I see stars and lay a hand on one of her horns as I would on a normal woman's head.

And then, at her deep, throaty moan, I remember how affected she was last night.

Even harder at the thought, I slowly stroke the hard, curiously smooth material of her horns at about the rhythm she uses to bob her head over me. As her voice lifts in a high whine of bliss, her tail trembles. When I go a little faster her eyes cross altogether, and I groan to arch my hips up into her mouth and fuck that welcoming throat.

After experimenting around, I find the upper left horn—one of the more curved ones—is apparently the most sensitive. I focus on petting it, choking on a gasp of bliss to see her lashing tail, finally unable to resist, curls around between her legs so she can tease herself with no hands. Both hers are occupied, one caressing my balls and the other teasing her own nipple. All the while that incredibly articulate tongue of hers twitches against my engorged member, unable to take full advantage of its talents when I'm down her throat.

The thought brings me right up to the edge already, but what really pushes me over in our morning quickie is the way the fast work of her tail provokes an orgasm in her, too. With a gag and a low, vibrating moan that tightens her throat, the demoness's eyes roll up into her head. She succeeds in pulling the orgasm out of me before I even realize what's happened. Moaning to receive my load, Baphomet swallows every drop before raising her head to look at me in a merry, mischievous way.

"Something to help you stay focused while you're at work, Master." She sighs to slide her tail out of herself, then prances up with a giddy smile. "I'll go get showered and leave for work, sir! We can't be seen together, after all. What would HR think?"

As she dances into the hall and blows me a kiss over her shoulder, I remain tangled in the sheets. Orgasm aside, I look and feel like a dead body after a bombing.

What in the world is going on here?

Somehow, everything seems stranger today than it did yesterday. Yesterday was such a breakneck day full of so much information that it had taken on a surreal quality at the time. Thinking of it now, it maintains that surreal quality in spades. My mind writhes in conflict with itself. All of this seems absolutely impossible…yet the evidence is right beneath me, right around me.

Somehow it felt so natural last night, when the

house—the nest—was in its blank state. Somehow, even though I don't know who I am or if she's even telling me the whole truth of any of this, I know that there's at least a little piece of accuracy to it in some way I can't tell.

And that thought is what keeps me in a state of constant disbelief.

The kitchen I have made for myself is sizable and stylish, dark tiling offset by the same view of the city I've seen while doing the dishes for…how long? How long have I lived in this place?

She's right. When I stop and think about my life, I really *don't* remember anything before yesterday. Oh, don't get me wrong. I remember general things. I remember the identities of my family members and all my coworkers at Helcom. I even have my fair share of childhood memories. I remember my favorite things, old addresses, my mother's phone number.

Yet, somehow, I feel dissociated from these memories. While I might remember them in a way that's like watching a film, I lack all hints of emotional tie when I play them back in my brain. In truth, I was never very sentimental before, but this is something else entirely. It's like I'm some other entity leaning into the back of my own skull, looking at all these memories that have been placed, as Beatrix said, just for context. Where once I felt rooted to my childhood, now, somehow, I realize I've always been rooted someplace else.

But where?

After figuring out the new coffee maker, I realize with a scoff that I could have just manifested myself a mug. That thought, in turn, inspires another. I glance at the wrinkled pack of cigarettes, now sitting on the edge of the sleek kitchen island instead of the dingy counter where I left them. When I look down at my hand, a new pack of black clove cigarettes is already there.

Damn! I smile fondly at the sight of the things. Reminds me of high school. They're a pain in the ass to get these days, and as I pull one out and light it amid the smell of brewing coffee, I sigh in satisfaction. "Tastes like Christmas," I say to myself.

A whole new chain of thought forms out of that. If I'm a demon lord, am I an enemy of God? I'm not really a religious person. I'm a practical man, concerned mostly with my own survival and success. From that perspective, it's better to take notions of religion and God out of this…at least for now. I have to look at the facts. The facts are, a demon wants to help me, or seems to. If she's telling the truth, there are angels willing to kill me.

So from a purely utilitarian perspective, until further notice I'm willing to put my faith in Baphomet.

Or Beatrix, rather. When she steps out of her bathroom with a smile on her slightly flushed face, her horns are missing and her demonic red eyes have softened to that lovely blue. In a set of black and red lingerie that has my blood aflame again, my loyal servant smiles at me and uses the towel around her neck to fluff her hair. "As always, sir, you have nice taste in architecture…and shower heads."

"Thanks." Sliding a mug of coffee to her, I ask, "If we're demons, shouldn't words like 'Christmas,' I don't know, make my eyes boil in my head or something?"

With a laugh, Beatrix leans against the island and sips the offered brew. "Of course not, Master…don't forget, demons are angels, too."

Nodding, I tap my cigarette out in the ashtray at my elbow. "And if I'm this demon lord, Vic Legion probably isn't my real name, huh?"

Smiling coyly, Beatrix shakes her head.

"And you're not going to tell me?"

"My tongue cannot pronounce it in this form, or any humanoid form," she says with a sad sigh, "and no humanoid ear may dare hear it and survive. The same is true of all celestial names…a pity, for I think if it did not kill your vessel its pronunciation would break all seven seals at once and bring you back to yourself right away."

Yeah, that's a shame in a sense…but, well, I have to admit that I'm pretty attached to this 'vessel.' We're talking about *me,* after all! My body, my self, my whole identity. Vic Legion. Given pause to hear this, I look at her carefully and ask, "Does this mean that when my identity fully returns to me, I won't be able to be myself anymore?"

"You'll be more yourself than you've ever been while trapped here as Vic," she tells me solemnly. "And by then you won't want to live a mundane humie existence anymore. You'll be free to do whatever pleases you. To rule again, in this form or any other."

Well…as long as I could still choose to become Vic Legion from time to time, I supposed that was all right. Still—sounded a lot like death. I tried not to think about it too much and focused instead on the issue of these seals. "So is this first seal broken?"

"The Seal of Sol is not yet completely destroyed, and will not be until all other seals are vanquished. As one approaches a seal-keeper, either geographically or by learning who they are, the power of the seal begins to fade: it can only be broken by defeating the keeper."

"In battle?"

"Among other things," she explains, setting down her coffee mug with a glance at the clock. Sliding the towel from around her shoulders, Beatrix goes on to say, "Any challenge, properly won, is sufficient to break a seal. Riddles are a common alternative to battle; the retrieval of precious objects; victory in a competition. There are many other means by which seals may be broken, many of which are dependent upon the nature of the seals themselves."

Nodding, I begin to tell her I understand, but I am immediately distracted by her lithe twirl. While her hair swings around her, it dries to a perfect wild finish, and by the time her spinning stops she wears a stylish pantsuit with a black and white striped top that makes her chest look extra emphasized.

"I'm off to work, Master," she says with a smile. "See you there! Try not to make it too obvious that we're fucking now."

While she springs off with a wink, I think to myself that she was the one staring at me yesterday, not the other way around…but, whatever. She turns me on, and as I watch her go all I can think is how much I look forward to fucking her again tonight.

Maybe.

After showering in a master bathroom whose dark tiles recall the kitchen, I shave, manifest myself a whole new wardrobe, and pick a sleek suit for the office. Dress for the job you want, they say. I straighten my tie, fix the cuffs of my sleeves, then adjust the tailored jacket in the mirror before heading out the door. There's no helping my faint grin of pride, I admit it.

I've just locked it behind me when Melody leans out, looking curiously shy at me.

"Hi, Vic," she says, one hand pressed to her heart, her soft lilac hair pulled up atop her head and braided ornately as a German mädchen. "Did you have a good night?"

"It was great," I say, whirling with a smile for her. I flip my keys back into my palm and stuff them in my pocket.

"Sorry again I had to dash."

"Oh, that's all right…I was going to see if you were interested in coming over tonight instead, but I thought I heard you come out earlier and…I didn't know you had a girlfriend."

There's a surprising amount of disappointment elegantly hidden in her smilingly said words. Damn! Rotten timing, Baphomet…could have shown up and revealed all these secrets to me any other week, when my cute neighbor wasn't finally starting to come out of her shell for me.

"Beatrix, you mean? Oh, no, she's not my girlfriend. She's, uh—" Think fast. "My sister."

Melody's eyes widen until I finally understand the cliché 'big as saucers.' "O—oh! My! So it's like that with you two, huh?"

Oblivious, I tell her, "Oh, yeah, she stays over sometimes…now that she's got a job at the same place I work, I expect she'll be sleeping at my place all the time now."

My neighbor's face is by now the darkest shade of red I've ever seen on a human. Was it something I said? "Gosh! I see! I had no idea."

"Yeah," I say, still clueless as I summon the elevator. "So dinner sounds nice! I'd love to. What time?"

Blinking her slightly glazed eyes, laughing in a nervous way, Melody wrings her hands and says, "Well, uh, if it's no imposition, maybe—maybe six?"

"Sounds great!" Feeling like a million bucks, I wink at her and step into the elevator that arrives to collect me. "Catch you later."

Is it just me, or was Melody a little odd back there? Was she getting shy again, or is there something up? Sniffing my own collar to find it fine, I shake it off and try to get in the mood for work.

Normally, such a thing is impossible. Helcom is a miserable place for miserable people, where engineers and salespeople and marketing execs all go to have their souls pulled out of their bodies. Today, though, I have to admit I'm feeling pretty great.

Which is probably why the check engine light comes on when I'm about halfway to work.

Well, that's what happens when you drive a vintage car through a cactus patch. To be honest, maintenance is overdue on her anyway. Making a mental note to get it checked out while I park in the company lot, I smooth my tie, clear my throat, and glance at my own reflection in the visor.

It seems to me that, if I want to embrace a new life and a new self—or an old self, rather—then I'd ought to act like this is my first day at Helcom all over again. Hence the suit, and the good attitude.

Hard to keep a good attitude when you step into such a rotten place, though. The gray walls are designed to stomp your spark dead. Trying not to let it get to me, I make my way down the hall, exchange a smoldering glance with Beatrix to somewhat counter the natural environment of the office, and make my way to my cubicle.

Before settling into work, I stick my head into Mike's office. "Did Gabe end up looking for me again yesterday?"

"Nah, he left early, too…hell!" Finally glancing away from his computer with a short laugh, Mike leans back in his seat and folds his hands over his ribs. "Swank duds! What's the occasion?"

"Just trying to adjust my attitude," I tell him with sincerity that's only a bit feigned. I really am tired of being so bored all the time; of sneaking around to avoid the ramifications of being bored. Why deal with all that crap when I could get competitive?

After all…if I'm really a demon lord, why settle for sitting around in a cubicle waiting to die? If I'm really so powerful, why can't I climb the corporate ladder all the way to the top, or maybe even find something better?

Draping my jacket over the back of my chair and booting up my laptop, I crack my knuckles and get to work on the last project I left off on. And I do work. But, with the distracting thought of Beatrix nearby and all the memories of Baphomet the night before, my mind is elsewhere as I do my job.

What time is it? Barely forty-five minutes into the day. I lean back in my chair and drum my pencil against the arm of my chair.

"I'm going for a smoke," I announce to Mike, who says with a quick locking keystroke, "I'll join you."

Soon we're on the patio by the back parking lot, consigned to the space of the smokers' shame. Among corporate workers, however, there are few ways to guarantee momentary peace quite as reliable as killing yourself with cigarettes.

Could I kill myself, though? I mean, I guess I could, since Baphomet had explained that there were those out to kill my mortal vessel. But…once whatever I truly am emerges from the shell of this body, what then? Will I ever be able to die?

I have so many questions.

So does Mike…not about me, though.

"So," he says, leaning in and sparing little more than a cursory glance at my curious cigarette, "how was, uh, dinner last night?"

"My guy—"

I laugh a little, rubbing my jaw and then my forehead while my brain flashes back through the night. The word

Master echoes through my head in her voice. I'm inundated in memories of her many acrobatic talents…and, well, the interest in saving my life. And the car accident.

Is this trauma?

"Let's just say I'm glad I went out," I summarize, earning an envious sigh and glance toward the building from my friend.

"I'll bet you are. Man! I just don't have that kind of confidence."

"You could…it's all a matter of perspective." I take a drag from the cigarette, which sparks and crackles as a clove pops amid the tobacco. "How you view yourself determines how others view you in this world. They say 'fake it 'till you make it,' and that's true…"

My eye is caught by the appearance of Gabe's face on the other side of the glass door to the patio.

Acrid, sweetly-scented smoke curls from my lips as I conclude, "…but the most important part is believing your own lie."

When the manager steps out, he's smiling. "Legion! Hello, Fisher."

Mike nods toward the manager with a glance at his smartwatch. "Five more minutes," he says with a nervous little laugh and a wave of the cigarette.

"I'm not trying to horn in…well, I guess I am a little, but only for Legion here. And since you're here on-time today"—he adds this with a punchably playful wink at me—"I don't see why you can't come back out and finish your break once we've had a word."

It'd be so easy to drive the car up the parking lot and run this asshole over, man. Repressing a sigh, I stub out the cigarette in the overloaded concrete ashtray. "Catch you at lunch," I tell Mike, which is a lie, because as soon as I'm back in my cube we'll be gossiping like old hens.

In the building, Gabe looks over me with approval and says, "I'm glad to see you took our talk yesterday more seriously than I expected you to!"

"Sorry I've let you develop such low expectations of me," I tell him. It occurs to me now that I really *have* let the people around me develop low expectations. I should call my mother back.

"It's nothing like that! I'm always sorry to give critical feedback, but it's very rewarding when people take it as intended."

Opening the door to his office while I glimpse Beatrix in profile—looking aggressively bored with the flirtation attempts of some humie colleague—Gabe ushers me in. The olive-skinned, gray-haired man inside turns from his study of a wall-mounted white board and smiles, offering his hand. "I just wanted you to meet our head of sales while he was still around this morning. This is Victor Legion, Raphael."

"Gabe's just been telling me about you this morning. Said you've got great people skills and that you find life in a cubicle a little too stifling."

"I wouldn't say 'no' to an office with a window I can see through," I tell him with a wink and nod to the view of the oak tree behind him.

Raphael laughs, his teeth bright white against his manicured beard. "Well, we usually reserve offices for our higher-ranking team members, but I don't see why you couldn't find your way to one sooner rather than later. You've certainly already dressed the part."

Smoothing my tie, I tell him, "I appreciate that…I do have to admit, though. View aside, I'm happy where I am."

"Now, don't be so quick to turn down an opportunity like this." Gabe nudges me in the arm. "Raphael here is an excellent manager and mentor, and—"

"I understand why he's hesitant. It's a whole new department, isn't it? You were just telling me he has no sales experience." Still with that beneficent smile, Raphael fishes a business card out of his shirt pocket and passes it over to me. While I imagine him putting a handful of little cards into his pocket every day like a soldier loading a gun, he says, "Why don't you think about it before committing to the transfer and let me know your decision in a few days?"

"Sure," I tell him, nodding. "It's mostly commission-based, right?"

"That's where the real money is, but there's a generous base salary, as well."

Still nodding, I tuck the card away in my wallet and instantly forget about it. "All right…I'll give it some thought. Maybe after the department thing on Friday I'll make my decision."

Looking even more pleased, Gabe raises his eyebrows. "You're coming?"

"Like I said, I'm thinking about it. Nice meeting you, Raphael, thanks for taking the time."

"Oh, it's a pleasure. I can tell just by talking to you that you'd be a great fit for the department. Here's to hoping you'll make the right choice!"

With another nod, now at Gabe, I add to him, "Thanks for introducing us," and leave the office feeling like a million bucks.

Always reassuring to go into a room thinking you're going to lose your job only to leave it feeling more valuable than you were before. What really is value in a place like this, though? Beatrix smiles secretively at me. I pass her desk, patting its grace surface as I do. The taste of her body returns to me with a shudder, and as I settle in my seat, I find myself once again thinking of the day and night before.

The rest of the day glides by smoothly, everything a pantomime of reality. While I play the part of Victor Legion, my mind races through what has happened to me. What has been revealed.

How insane this all sounds! I feel like these are the types of thoughts and experiences most cult leaders probably have, or think they're having. There's no doubt that Beatrix views me with the starry eyes of an acolyte for her leader.

But isn't that all just another trap? It would be easy to get distracted from the task of breaking these seals, whatever they are, when developing a following and getting embroiled in some kind of religious practice. Then, without achieving my immortal form, I'd be just another Jim Jones. A blip in history, if that.

Nah…that's not me. Frankly, I haven't really ever had ambitions of being part of history, and I still don't. But the idea of having a kind of quiet, all-expansive power—that appeals to me more the more I think about it through the day. In truth, it seems like if I really am a powerful demon lord of some kind, the best thing would be to appear as a mortal and keep all those powers on the down-low.

But something is wrong now, for sure. After having it pointed out to me, it seems like some kind of truth. The whole of society is oppressive and laden with distractions.

Is this all to keep me from becoming aware of my situation and navigating my way out of the trap? Are the angels aware of the man I've been incarnated as?

I contemplate the car chasing me while on my way back to my apartment building. Is that driver an angel of some kind? And the woman on the overpass—is she part of the quartet, the choir of women who evidently serve me?

There's been so much to ask and so much to know that I'm not even sure we talked about the car chase. Maybe Beatrix already knows and doesn't have to be told? I'm not sure. I would check with her…but, before any of that, I want to focus on Melody. The timing seems bad, but if I can change my attitude about work, maybe I can change my attitude about that, too.

After freshening up and ditching the jacket, I look around the kitchen for space. The third time I turn around, one of the walls has expanded a little. A new glass-front door stands beside the sizable pantry. I open the wine cabinet to find it stocked and smile to myself. Who cares about a commission? Who cares about work? Maybe I'll quit Helcom altogether…then hunt down those clowns with the seals and make myself ruler of the fucking universe.

Emperor Legion.

Yeah.

I like the sound of that.

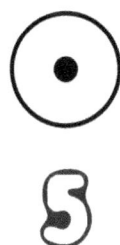

5

MANIFESTED WINE IN-HAND, I knock on the door of the apartment across the hall and loosen my tie a bit. Melody opens it a few seconds later, her features brightening with delight to see me. "Vic," she says, her voice soft and happy as the dimples pressing into her flushed cheeks.

"Hey, Melody...thank you for inviting me. Sorry if I'm a little early."

"No, it's fine!" As she pushes wider the door of her apartment to reveal a much nicer foyer than my old one, with a dark wood floor and a bookshelf visible in the hall as one steps toward the living room, I find myself much more taken with her somehow bridal appearance. Maybe it's the white dress whose short sleeves fall crisply ironed against her pale arms, or the happy yellow apron that makes her seem so domestic and gentle. She has such a comforting presence that I momentarily forget the madness of my life and what I'm supposed to be.

As she accepts the wine, she tells me, "I'm still in the middle of cooking, but—"

"Can I help?"

"Oh, gosh, well, you probably can...let's see..."

After I've been set up at a cutting board and she's got a couple of glasses of wine poured, Melody stands beside me to monitor the stove. She pushes a stray lock behind the pink-tinted curve of her ear, saying, "I'm so excited to finally have you over!"

"'Finally!'" Laughing, shaking my head, I cut the radish flowers in emulation of the one she's shown me and assure her, "I've been the one trying to invite you over...you just seem so nervous and so eager to get out of conversations that I wasn't sure it would be a good idea."

That bashful look I love to see her wear is back. Her eyes lower. "It's nothing like that. It's just—oh, I don't know."

"What is it?"

"Nothing! It'll sound silly if I say it."

"Well now I'm really curious."

"You just seem like such a 'cool guy,' I guess...I never would have thought you'd want to give me the time of day."

"Are you kidding? You're beautiful." While I glance over in time to see her lips part and her blush deepen, I continue, "And you seem smart, and kind...what do you do for a living?"

"Oh! I, um—I'm a student, actually. Getting my Master's in education."

My eyebrows lift. "This is a pretty nice place for a

student—ah—"

A covered pot trembles as its contents begin to overboil. While she switches off the heat, I grab a paper towel from the nearby sink's edge. She blots at it with a shake of her head, saying, "I'm so clumsy! Sorry, I'm usually a much better cook…you've gotten me all distracted."

"Or you've let yourself get distracted, anyway…I'll be strict with you about it later," I tell her with a wink, earning a gasp and a slap of my bicep. Her eyes, though, flutter across mine and then away while she fights back her blushing grin.

"You're really a cad…just the sort of person I imagined you'd be."

"So you imagine me, do you?"

The pinkish tips of her ears darken with embarrassment (and excitement, I suspect) as Melody looks rapidly around for her oven mitt. She shuts off the timer just as it finishes, saying in a nervous lilt, "Oh, look! Dinner is done."

I have to hand it to her—she's a little shy and pretty clumsy, but Melody is a superb cook. While we eat dinner she asks me about myself and my family life, my job, all the things people in our situation normally ask one another. We should have done this sooner. Here I've been starving to death across the landing, surviving on a combination of take-out, ramen, and sweets from my mother when all this time there's been a Michelin chef waiting to feed me. I tell her about as much once I've helped her do the dishes and am about two and a half glasses of wine into the bottle.

"Oh, that? That was nothing." She laughs and shakes her head. "Cooking is easy. It's just about following instructions, and being willing to try again when you've failed."

"You haven't seen me in the kitchen."

Giggling, Melody tells me, "I guess that's true."

Her face changes, however, and she presses her wineglass to her shoulder. "Oh, but you've got your sister living there now, right? Is she much of a cook?"

"I don't think so," I tell her, failing to imagine Beatrix doing anything in the kitchen other than setting off the fire alarm. Though I don't know her well enough to judge her on that level, I get the sense that the concerns of demons are pretty far removed from domestic spheres of humie life. Not to mention, well…with sex as an energy source, I'm not even sure if she has a need to eat at all. Will the same be true of me someday? "She's got other interests than cooking."

"I can't imagine how anybody can live without cooking or baking *something* every once in awhile, even if they mostly do take-out…that kind of food bill will be high with the two of you living together, you know." I use my wine glass to hide my smile at her remonstration. She goes on, "You should really both consider learning a few basic meals and taking turns for dinners."

"Maybe you could come over and teach us a thing or two."

"That might be fun. Oh, but…" She blushes so easily! I don't understand it this particular time, though. Especially as she says, "I don't want to horn in on you."

"What do you mean? It wouldn't be horning in. She's my sister, after all."

"So it's—open?"

"Open?"

She nods, waiting for me to answer.

I look at her in confusion, then suddenly piece it all together in a snap that leaves my face bright red.

"Wh—what are you saying?"

Her face even brighter than mine, Melody gasps. "I thought you were saying this morning that you and your sister—"

"What! No!"

"Oh! But I thought I heard—last night—"

My mouth hangs open as my brain replays all the moaning, screaming, banging, coming, and going that occurred last night. The mental camera then pans through the walls of my magically up-sized apartment and into Melody's, where my poor neighbor lies awake, eyes wide at the animal sounds coming from the opposite end of the floor.

Seeing my expression, Melody's develops a look of something like panic. "I'm so sorry to listen in," she says quickly. "I really didn't mean to be rude. It's just…these walls are so thin, and…"

"Wait a minute." My arm slides along the back of the couch, where it rests behind her as I lift my eyebrows. "Do you mean to say that when I bring women home to have sex, you can hear it?"

The Grecian column of her neck is as flushed as her cheeks. Melody reflexively covers it with a delicate hand. "I mean…sometimes I try to put on music, but…"

Walls rattling with the banging of a headboard. Moans emanating from my apartment door. Giggling girlfriends saying good-bye on their ways downstairs in the morning.

"'Sometimes' you put on music," I say, leaning into it by teasing her, "but other times you listen, huh?" While she balks, I grin and go on. "No wonder you're so shy around me."

I finish my wine in one brisk swallow and lean toward the coffee table, where I set my empty glass. Hers held defensively before her slim bosom, Melody says with a gasp, "I really try *not* to listen!"

"Uh-huh, sure…that's why you're so embarrassed right now."

With a quick set of motions, I slide my arm down from the couch and tighten it around the cool small of her back. While she gasps in a mixture of fright and excitement, I remove the glass from her hands and set it aside without looking from her face.

"Do you like what you hear when you listen in on me, Melody?"

"Oh!" Moaning, her lips parting in shock, Melody trembles in my arm and stares fearfully into my eyes. "I just get embarrassed. I don't want to invade your privacy."

"But you do. That's okay, though…I like to get loud." My free hand raises to caress her cheek, framing her jaw with thumb and forefinger. She gazes into my eyes with her own emerald green ones softened by desire. "What about you, Melody? Do you like to get loud?"

"I don't know," she whispers. While I let my fingers trail down her throat, I glance down in admiration and find her nipples strain against the thin fabrics of her bra and dress. Looking back up into her face, I permit my caress to traverse over one tense peak. Her breath hitches in a gasp and she looks almost disbelieving, her body wiggling against mine.

"What do you mean, you don't know?"

"I mean—I've never—"

My eyes widen. "No way. Are you a virgin?"

Nervously nodding, she admits, "I don't really…do things like that. Or like this. But—but since I've moved in…"

Her breath hitches again as my hand trails down, down, following the wonderful line of her waist to the slight flare of her hip. While I slowly gather the fabric of her dress she glances down, but doesn't protest. Focused on my eyes again, she continues in a whisper, "Since I've moved in and heard you with all these women, I've become so…so curious. They sound like they're enjoying themselves so much—enjoying *you* so much."

Having shortened the length of her dress enough to do so with ease, I caress her thigh and marvel at the chilled marble of her flesh. She needs warming up, poor girl. While my hand edges higher and higher along the underside of her thigh, soon enough making tickling contact with the lacy edge of her panties, Melody continues.

"I want to know what it's like to feel that way…want to know *what* they're feeling to make those sounds at all."

As my hand slides up to cup her plump but delicate rear through her panties, I arch a brow. "Surely you can imagine it."

"I told you," she whispers. "I've never done anything like that before."

With new, more astonished understanding, I look at her as if she's grown a second head. "You can't possibly mean you've never even touched yourself, right?"

But that's just what she means. I can see it in the aversion of her eyes and the way she rests her hand on her head with an embarrassed whine. "I knew you would think I'm strange! I've just never—it feels so naughty. I can't stand to feel like such a dirty girl, but…but hearing those women you bring around…"

"Makes you want to be a dirty girl, too, huh?"

Lowering her hand to cover her eyes, she whispers, "Maybe."

"Maybe…maybe…" I take that wonderful hand in mine and kiss its pearly knuckles. "Maybe you need to admit what you want, Melody…are you saying you want me to teach you how to fuck?"

Moaning at my language, Melody slowly nods.

"Yes," she whimpers, "yes, please…I want you to touch me the way you touch those other women…I want to learn how you make them scream like that, so uninhibited and wild…"

My blood heated by the neighbor from whom I'd expected a fling and little more, I begin to see a potential for a long and fulfilling affair. Eyes on hers, I lower her innocent hand between her thighs. She gasps, her mouth remaining open as I gently press her fingertip to the damp cameltoe of her own cotton panties.

"I think first, before I can show you how I pleasure a woman, you need to learn how to pleasure yourself… here…"

Releasing her hand, I draw her panties down her thighs and yield a groan from both of us. The tidy patch of hair upon her mound is silvery, and her untested vulva is swollen with desire based on our talk alone. With her revealed, I draw her into my lap and let her hear my sigh of pleasure as her bare ass fits to my straining prick.

"Oh," she gasps, "Vic, oh…I'm so embarrassed…"

"It's fun to be embarrassed with someone you trust, though. And, besides…you've listened in on me whenever you've felt like it. Consider this your just desserts." While I push her leg wider, she bites her lip and looks down at herself in my lap.

"Go on," I tell her, stroking her thigh. "I want to see you touch yourself for me, Melody."

Moaning softly, Melody looks reluctantly into my face for a few long seconds. Then, with a shy glance at herself, she begins to pet the splayed valley. The fever sweeping over me is nearly overwhelming: I stroke her leg to keep myself from helping her.

"There," I tell her while she gasps softly, "isn't that nice…"

"Yes!" Her fingers graze naturally toward her clit, where she almost yelps. "Oh—it's so sensitive though…"

"Good…play with your clit, Melody, I want to see it… want to hear you whine…feels so good it almost hurts, doesn't it?"

"Uh-huh…uh-huh…oh, Vic…it makes me so excited when you watch me…"

"Do you get this wet when you're listening to me fuck my guests?"

"Oh, umm…yes, yes—Vic, I get wetter…"

"Well…that's a nice thought, because you're awfully wet now."

I just can't resist. The tip of my finger trails up her thigh and probes toward her labia, drawing them apart to slide deeper against the trench. All the honey of lust that's pooling there causes my finger to slide effortlessly over her silky folds, and while she moans in astonished pleasure I tell her, "You should touch yourself like this the next time you hear me giving a girlfriend a good, hard fucking…or you could come over and play with us. But, I admit, the thought of you teasing that cute little pussy to the sound really makes me want to get loud."

"Mm—oh, oh, Vic, ah! Your finger, it feels so good—ah!"

I gently nudge hers aside and let her feel the benefit of my experience. While drawing my well-lubricated finger back and forth over her most sensitive nub, I press a kiss to her unaccustomed mouth. She moans, writhing, permitting access to my tongue while my finger works her to a higher state of ecstasy every second. My cock throbs in my pants while she grinds her rear against me, her hips arching to increase the pressure of my touch. I keep it gentle but steady, rolling her to her first orgasm while we exchange passionate, breathless kisses flavored like wine and good cooking.

"I feel so strange," whimpers Melody against me soon, "oh, oh, Vic, I feel odd—"

"Just relax into it, baby…that's right, just let me take you there. Just relax, just relax…oh, yes—"

Her face changes sharply in an instant, her body arching and hips pushing up against my fingers. While her moans raise to fill her apartment, I grin into Melody's face and steadily guide her through her orgasm. One fingertip poises at the entrance of her virgin cunt to feel her quiver, the greedy pulses of her pussy making my cock twitch with lust. The beatific expression of her face and the long, almost pained tones of her moans…ah, I could look at her all day. And night.

"There you go," I tell her softly, slowing my caresses as her orgasm ends. "Worth the wait?"

"Ah—ah—oh, uh-huh, oh…"

"That's good…"

After one last, long kiss, I slide her from my lap and fix her dress. "Now," I tell her, staring into her face, "I'm going to leave you alone for the night and go back home to fuck Beatrix." While Melody moans at the thought, I reach between her legs to tease her a little more. "She's not my sister…but you didn't mind thinking that she was, huh?"

"Oh—oh, mm, who is she, then?"

"A hot, crazy girl who wants to be my sex slave."

My answer merits a gasp that makes me grin. Toying with her clit a little faster now, seeing the glaze of desire still in her eyes, I ask, "You want to be my sex slave, too, Melody? Want me to come over here and use you whenever I feel like it?"

Panting, Melody bites her lip and says, "But won't she be mad?"

"Nah…she's a good girl. I'm sure she'd like to hear you enjoying yourself over here as much as you like to listen to us over there. You dirty girl…well, I'll be damn sure to give you something worth listening to tonight."

With one last kiss, I stand up, smilingly tell her, "Thanks for dinner," and make my way toward the hall.

"Wait," she says, sitting up with a gasp.

I pause.

"Maybe, um…maybe you and your—friend could come over for dinner sometime? Like, I don't know… maybe this Monday?"

"Sounds like it could be fun…I'll let you know if something comes up."

Blowing a kiss to the flustered girl, I let myself out into the hall and grin. Damn. Here I thought I was good with women before…Beatrix seems to have made me even better. I let myself into the apartment, prepared to call out to her, but before I can even do that she comes trotting from the living room in another lingerie get-up, her horns revealed and her flaming wings flickering behind her.

"Welcome home, Master," she says, elegantly kneeling before me. Her smiling gaze finds mine, then changes. She looks at me in a very strange way, her head tilting. "Where have you been, may I ask, sir?"

"Dinner with a friend."

Drawing Beatrix to her feet by her bicep, I kiss her at once. She moans, especially when I take her hand and press it to the front of my trousers. While I push her back against the break wall between the kitchen and the hallway, Baphomet moans and eagerly rubs my erection.

"Mm, Master! Oh, you're so exceptionally hard…"

"We need to be nice and loud so Melody across the hall can hear it…she's too shy to come and spend time with us, so we'll have to go over there if we want to include her. But—it seems that she liked what she heard last night."

Moaning, the demoness pulls my zipper down and frees my straining member. I gasp her human name while she tugs it, and all the while I ease my hand into her black thong to find her soaking wet.

"What a slut you are for your master…I barely need to touch you to get you ready for me."

"Oh, yes, sir! Yes, I'm a happy little whore for you…" While her lashing tail whips wildly against the wall, I prop her up against the bar. One leg drapes around my waist as I guide my dick to her dripping hole. I tease her while she whimpers, "Please, please, I can't live without your cum…oh, I need to be used by you every day, all the time…please, please put it in me! Please fuck me, Master!"

"Louder," I command, freeing her tits from her bodice and savaging one nipple with kisses.

"Please!" Genuinely desperate, Beatrix clutches at my shirt with both hands. Her voice raises in an absolutely insane scream that makes me twitch with want. "Please, Master, please, use me! Fuck me, fuck me until it hurts, oh, I'm so horny!"

"You sure are," I say, grabbing hold of one of those sharp ornaments protecting her skull. At the same time, I ram my length home into her body. She screams out loud, the stimulation so overwhelming that she cums on the spot. Her tongue lolls out and her eyes roll up toward her brow while I fuck her through one demonic orgasm and directly into another.

"Ha, ha, ha, yes! Master! Yes, oh, fuck, I'm not worthy,

I'm not worthy!"

"I love the way you beg," I tell her, lifting my head to kiss her mouth before nipping down the line of her throat. "I think I'll make you do it all the time, all the time—"

"Oh yes, yes, yes, fuck, please!"

I realize that, incredibly, she seems to be having a third orgasm, and I hurry my caresses of her horn to bring on the next. Demon women are really something else! Don't get me wrong, Melody is gorgeous…but is she a supernatural woman equipped with the ability to have supernatural sex?

Frankly, I'm noticing a difference about myself. Maybe it's just because I'm in the apartment, where the rules of physics themselves seem to be bent, but I have a strength I've never before perceived. A virility, too. My endurance is beyond any normal human limit, and while the demoness in my arms is blinded by ecstasy, I feel like I could keep pounding into her for days.

If Melody hadn't gotten me incredibly turned on by blowing my expectations so out of the water, I probably *could* keep going for days.

As ready as I was by the time I left her apartment, though, Baphomet's begging pussy has me in dire straits sometime around her ninth orgasm. As her tail wraps around my arm and her leg grips me more intently, I slam home into her one final set of times and squeeze her horn for good measure. She groans, her head rolling back against the bar, her body rapidly fluttering around mine as she enjoys her tenth and final orgasm of the evening. My climax pulses into her while she pants, those almost translucent eyelids twitching like her pussy.

I kiss her, slide out of her, and catch her as her knees collapse beneath her.

"Thank you, sir," she whispers dimly, barely able to catch her breath.

Grinning, I kiss her lower lip, run my hand over her breast, then help her pull up her panties before my cum can run down her leg. "You're welcome, slave…"

While she moans with pleasure, I give her nipple a sharp little tug until she's clinging to my belt. "So greedy…I need to get some sleep tonight, slut, so try to resist until tomorrow…"

Whimpering like a kicked puppy, Baphomet pouts until I tell her, "But on Monday, we both have an invitation to dinner with Melody across the hall there… and that should be very fun."

A wicked grin unfurling across her flushed face, my demonic helper nods in agreement. "Yes, Master, that does sound very fun. I saw that pretty girl this morning… she looked at me with such disappointment, not knowing how happy I would be to fuck her with you." Though at first she giggles, Baphomet soon pouts. "But she consorts with an angel," says the demon grimly.

I arch a brow. "How can you tell?"

"The same way I found you, Master, sticking out like a sore thumb in Helcom. There are energy signatures in the world, celestial and infernal, which are passively produced while an angel or demon metabolizes energy for magical purposes. Individuals produce these signatures, and so do the buildings they own or control. Your nest, for example. Helcom, too. And that girl's apartment radiates celestial energy."

Tapping my chin, I tell her, "Well, she said something about it being her aunt's…who knows. Say—that reminds me. Before I got home yesterday and found you here…"

As Baphomet's eyes lose their hazy veneer of lust and instead widen with sharp horror, I relate the anecdote about the car chase and its unexpected ending.

"You should have told me this sooner, Master!"

"Sorry," I tell her dryly, "I was a little overwhelmed by, you know, remembering I'm a demon lord and whatever."

Lips pursing, fingers drumming upon her chin, Baphomet looks at me with serious concern. "And you didn't see who was in the car?"

"No. But this dark-haired girl—was she one of the choir?"

After a few seconds of thought, Baphomet shakes her head. "That doesn't sound like one of my sisters," she says.

Her hand then lands flat upon my chest. She gazes earnestly into my eyes, her whole demeanor radiating true concern. Maybe this is why I have so little doubt in this whole situation. Baphomet is so much more genuine than I ever would have expected a sex-crazed demon to seem.

"You must be careful," says Baphomet. "Angels are everywhere, and they are more than willing to kill you… especially as you become more and more powerful. Please keep me abreast of wherever you go, sir."

"I will," I tell her, patting her hand before sliding past her into the kitchen for a drink. Wait—no, that's right. Stopping halfway, I choose to manifest one instead. Pleased with myself, I turn to her with a beer in my hand and though I offer it to her, she shakes her head. I keep it for myself, going on.

"Trust me: the last thing I want is to wind up dead just after learning such extraordinary things about myself. As embarrassing as it is for someone to let unlimited power make them a shut-in, I'm going to try to keep my head as low as I can…though I've got some obligations this week. Have to take the car into the garage tomorrow after the problem yesterday, and Friday is that work thing…"

Sighing, I shake my head and take a swig of beer at the mere thought. "I told the boss I'd consider it, but I don't think I'll be going."

Baphomet, however, has different ideas. Gasping, she catches my free hand and says, "But this is a perfect opportunity, Master!" As I arch my brow, she goes on, "It's like I was just saying. Helcom *overflows* with celestial energy. It's so all-encompassing that it's impossible to tell who's angelic and who's mortal when they're in that building. If I can see a few people in a different environment, though…that may very well help me narrow it down. You should certainly go! Act like you're introducing me to people…I'll be able to take a close look at them and get a sense for what they are inside based on how they talk to me."

"And they won't get suspicious if I introduce you around like you're my girlfriend? There's still HR to think about."

"Well, maybe tomorrow sometime I'll come out during one of your smoke breaks. We can act like we're just talking for the first time…that can be kind of hot, too, huh?"

This demoness is really going to get me into trouble one of these days. Nodding dumbly, I say, "Uh-huh."

With a long smile, Baphomet curls a lock of my hair around her finger, shudders with pleasure to touch me, and leans upon her toes to kiss my mouth. When her lips pull away from mine, they curve into a smile.

"Don't worry, Master. One way or another, we'll get you back to normal."

THE NEXT MORNING, after another sensual wake-up from my new servant—a title that still rings in my head with surreal astonishment—I take the car to an autobody shop not far from downtown. There's a breakfast place nearby. I stop and have a bite, hoping that by the time I'm done they'll have at least given me an estimate for when I can pick up the car.

Or maybe I can have Beatrix teleport there and pick it up on my behalf.

Now *that's* demon lord thinking.

Yes, my thinking has been changing. It's very strange. While I've never been the most responsible person, I like to think of myself as 'good.' At least...I thought I did.

But when you've got a hot succubus sex slave who's insanely devoted to you, and you also have the ability to manifest anything you want within the boundaries of your inter-dimensional apartment, and there's all these promises of more powers still to come—what does being good even matter? I ask myself that all through breakfast and, for some reason, find myself giving the waitress a bigger tip than usual at the end of the meal.

The restaurant was too fast. My car hasn't even been looked at by the time I'm through. Hostage, I take it gracefully, tell them I'll call later, then think about texting Mike for a ride. When I see the time, I decide to walk to the bus station downtown and take the bus line up instead. It's a beautiful morning bright and clear, and I'd rather stretch my legs before it gets too hot than twiddle my thumbs in front of the garage while waiting for my friend to come.

Tucson is an interesting city but, as mentioned, poorly laid out and incredibly confusing unless you know it well. This goes double for downtown. It's easy to get turned around in the city. It's easy to get lost, or lose someone.

And it's easy to miss somebody following you, unless you're already living in a state of heightened paranoia.

I don't notice the person at first, mostly because they're behind me. But after seeing this Caucasian person in a hooded sweatshirt reflected in not one or two but five different shop windows, I find myself unconsciously quickening my pace.

My pursuer also quickens their pace.

Now I'm gritting my teeth and thinking of Monday's car chase. Fantastic. What the hell is it now?

Baphomet was right. I need to be careful. I think about calling her, but I don't want this person to know any of my associates, either. Can't demons have some kind of telepathy, or something? Just for emergencies?

When the street seems open except for the person behind me and a few navigable bystanders, I stop and whip around.

Before I'm even facing them, they've done the same and darted into the nearest alley.

I scoff, calling, "Hey," as I sprint after them. My heart pounds in my ears. Is this the person from the car the other day? There are no vehicles creeping around that I can see. I have to catch them before they disappear and accordingly hurry my sprint.

But by the time I'm in the alley, they've got a ski mask on in the middle of a Tucson morning.

I duck his first punch, a wide cross I barely evade. Judging by the size of my opponent and the shape of the fist that just missed me, this is a guy. Bet he owns a Benz, too—though there's no time to ask. With another set of jabs, I'm left defending myself.

And I have to admit, I'm pleasantly surprised.

Though I'm not in terrible shape, I've never been much of a fighter. Didn't get into any hallway brawls in high school, didn't have much need to defend myself from bullying. The brunt of my understanding of basically any kind of combat comes from fiction, whether video games or martial arts movies.

So imagine my surprise when I catch one of this guy's jabs in my open hand.

Now I understand why they call them martial arts. Just like with engineering, creative, or any other design, there is a kind of collaborative production within the flow of a battle. Here the message is being portrayed in a platform of bodies, but it's a message all the same. And that message is, very simply, "You need putting in your place."

Let the greater artist win.

I am no great artist, but I find the same intuition that serves me in my work now rises to tell me block here, duck now, throw a kick in here and here. My blows are not artful or seasoned, but they are effective. Much as my ineptitude at chess once permitted me a victory over a cousin who prized his understanding of the game's strategy, (one of those free-floating memories that seem mine only in a vague, numb way), my inexpert blows delivered in unpredictable ways seem to stagger my opponent if only out of confusion.

In this way, I get a good shot right in his face.

He hisses, stumbling back amid the crack of bone. The blow wounds me, too—I can almost feel my knuckles bruise on the impact—but I shake it off and lift my fists for another set of jabs.

"You want some more, or are you going to tell me why you were stalking me today? Monday, too, right?"

Panting, one hand still pressed to his wounded eye, my opponent looks at me through his good one.

Someone else barrels into me from behind and slams me face-first into the dirty ground of the alley.

While I start to shout, the interloper covers my mouth with one burly hand. A Black man, apparently. Really narrows it down…couldn't he have a scar or a missing finger or something?

I try to bite and get a punch in the back of the head. As I see stars, my initial stalker staggers to his feet and reaches into his hooded sweatshirt.

Outside the alley, a car skids to a halt and honks its horn.

My attackers make a set of displeased noises in a language I don't recognize. As a car door opens, they dart in separate directions: one down the alley, one around the corner. That one shoves past the woman who hurries into the alley. She catches herself against the wall as the assailant flees, narrowly avoiding joining me on the ground.

"Asshole," she calls sharply after him, hurrying over to kneel beside me. "Hey, are you all right?"

"I think so…just a little scraped up."

After glancing at my bloodied palms and bruised knuckles, I look up at the woman who saved me.

And I find out that she's actually saved me twice.

"I know you," I say.

Peering down at me from behind sunglasses, the woman from the overpass pushes a few strands of dark hair back behind her ear. She leans down and slides her hands under my arms to help me up without hurting my hands.

"No you don't," she answers while I stand, "but I know you, Legion."

"May I ask how?"

"Let's talk on the way to my house," she says, heading to her car. "We can get you patched up there."

The common wisdom is to avoid getting in cars with strangers…but, well, there's an exception to every rule. With a glance at my palms, I say to myself, "Guess I'd better call in sick today, anyway," and make my way over to the door she unlocks for me.

Soon, while she cruises up to the foothills of Tucson—where affluent people (often longtime employees of Helcom and other corporations) look down on the city from their miniature desert mansions—my rescuer introduces herself.

"My name is Despina," she says, "and I know who you really are."

"Batman?"

"A wise-ass," she says with a brisk dart of dark eyes my way. While I roll down the window to light a cigarette and she disguises a look of supreme displeasure, she continues on. "I'll take it from the recent attempts on your life that you are already aware of your identity?"

Looking at her more carefully now, understandably suspicious after the events of the morning, I buy time with a drag on my cigarette. "Anybody who's not aware of their own identity has more problems than random people trying to kill them, Despina."

"You don't have to lie to me. Look."

Reaching back with one hand, Despina draws her hair away from her bronze skin. I lean over to see the small sigil tattooed behind her right ear, five marks of some kind all enclosed in a circle and a star-like network of lines. I don't have time to observe it closely before she goes on to say, "I'm part of an organization that exists on your behalf, Legion—or, at least, on behalf of the thing inside you."

"The true me," I agree, earning a glance of relative relief from her.

"Yes," she says. "The you whose dynamic tension against the forces of good makes this world a reality."

I rub my jaw, considering that sentiment. "That's giving me a lot of power."

"You *have* a lot of power. That's why the angels are trying to kill you before you can gain more. They understand what we do—that once you wake up, it's only a matter of time before their hold on you is completely obliterated."

"What is this group of yours, exactly? A cult?"

She shakes her head. "It's secular, though people try to call us a cult. Really, we're the result of an extrapolation of simulation theory."

Thinking on my conversation with Beatrix only a few days prior, I say, "I've heard of that. The idea that we're all living in some kind of computer simulation, right?"

"No. Not right. It's all a metaphor, not a literal

interpretation of the phrase. We're not just living in a videogame right now, for instance. This is all real…but it's fabricated, too."

"I think I can see why people get you guys mixed up with cultists."

"That *is why*. Because after scientific and philosophical thought reaches a certain point, it sounds like mysticism. But it's true. Look…you understand, right? That you're a demon of great power?"

Done fooling around, I simply say, "Yes."

"Then you probably also understand that your existence in this body is almost like a prison sentence. It's your jumpsuit and your term all rolled into one. The rest of this world is the prison…but the problem is that to have a prison, you have to have people. Real people. Real people who will die if the prison is destroyed—which would happen if its only prisoner is killed."

"But I don't understand. If I'm a prisoner to this system, this simulated world controlled by the angels, why didn't they just kill me when I was a kid?"

"It's the "time traveler killing baby Hitler" paradox… you hadn't done anything wrong when you were a kid."

"I haven't done anything wrong *now*, except remember."

"And by remembering," she explains, flicking a grim look over at me, "you are violating the physical laws of this world. That is what you are doing wrong. To stop you from violating more, they will now destroy you."

"And the seals—what, exist in such a great number so that angels have many chances to kill me?"

"That sounds right."

Lips pressed then, I hit the cigarette again while admiring Despina's whipping hair. "You really think they would destroy the world if they killed me?"

"There would be no reason for it to exist," she says

simply. "Without the primordial struggle of this reality and the moral tension presented by your existence, there's nothing to hold the world together."

That thought is very strange. I think of what little I do know of religion, of angels and demons—of stories about the Devil leading a rebellion against God and being cast down into the pits of the Earth. I wonder out loud to Despina, "Just how important of a demon lord *am* I?"

While turning into a small but affluent neighborhood off the highway, she arches a brow, then looks back at the road.

"Maybe you really *don't* know," she says under her breath.

"No," I tell her. "I really don't."

"Well…you're a pretty big deal, rest assured."

"If I'm so powerful, why didn't they just kill me when they had me on the ropes? Why put me here instead of annihilating me and saving themselves the trouble?"

She shakes her head while hitting the garage door button on the roof of her car. The vehicle slows to a cruise and she rolls up into the driveway. "There's much that, as humans, we just don't know. What little we do know is lacking in detail but vital in importance."

"And how *do* you know what you know?"

"A wide variety of sources. Apocryphal books of the Bible, suppressed scientific research from the Cold War, the secret writings of mad Arabs…the usual."

Good enough for me. The truth is that I don't really care how this fringe group of humies knows what they know. As long as they're on my side—that's what counts. While she shuts the garage door behind us and slides her sunglasses off, Despina studies me with those rich, dark eyes of hers.

"Let's get you patched up," she says, opening her door

with the flick of a wrist.

Like most foothill homes, Despina's is well-sized and finely decorated. It's even fit with a pool in the backyard, which gives me some good ideas for home renovations of my own…and raises some questions. If I were to, say, manifest a balcony with an infinity pool that overlooked the city, would it be invisible? Would I be able to throw something over the edge, or would it bounce off an invisible wall? Would pigeons be unable to shit on the deck? All good questions for Baphomet this evening.

For now, Despina leads me to a comfortably-sized art deco bathroom and encourages me to perch against the edge of the clawfoot tub.

"This is a beautiful place," I tell her, looking around while she fetches a first-aid kit from her medicine cabinet. "Have you been here long?"

"Only a few months," she answers, soaking a washcloth in warm water before bringing it and the kit to my side. "Let's see the damage."

I show her my palms. While she winces and holds one of my hands in hers, turning it this way and that, I tease, "My third day as a demon and I'm already riffing off the wounds of Christ…how's that for being a natural?"

Smirking, she gently wipes at bits of debris stuck in the scrapes. While I hiss into the sting of the warm cloth, she observes, "You've been a demon your whole life, though…you just haven't known it. Really? Only three days? Man, your head must be spinning."

"Like you wouldn't believe. I had a hot demon girl show up at my work and start telling me all this…I thought she was crazy. She started calling me things like 'Master' right away…"

Though I chuckle a little at the thought and she does, too, a hint of blush meanders across Despina's cheeks.

I glance casually away and tell her, "Not that I care, of course…she's incredibly sexy. Doesn't mind other women, either."

"O—oh yeah? That must be common with demons, huh…"

"I guess so." While she briefly sets the cloth aside to pluck up some ointment she deftly applies, I admire the curve of her neck and let my gaze follow it to the faint shadow of her cleavage. "You know, Despina, you're pretty brave to have me around to your house with nobody around."

"Not so brave to help somebody," she says, turning her blushing face from me to grab some gauze and a bandage wrap. As she applies them both with the expert hand seen in former athletes or current paramedics, she adds, "I guess I believe in the basic goodness of your human vessel."

"Do you really think my human vessel would be good, Despina?"

Her eyes flicker briskly up to me. She tucks the end of the bandage into the wrap and begins the process on my second hand, starting with the washcloth again. Is it me, or is her breathing a little heavier?

"I think your human vessel still has human priorities, at least," she tells me, wiping a little more swiftly with this second hand, applying the ointment a bit more slapdash. I savor every second of her reactions, wondering if it's arousal or unease or both coming off of her. "It wouldn't be wise for you to lose an ally by hurting or killing me… and it wouldn't exactly be helpful to your cause for you to get thrown in prison for one of those things, either. I guess, with those thoughts in mind, I trust your human self will be more loyal than your demon self will be impulsive or treacherous."

"Well," I tell her as she lays some gauze on my second hand, "rest assured, I won't betray you after you did a thing like help me today…and the other day, too. It's good to know there's a woman around town who has my back."

"I would do anything to protect this world."

"What makes you think I'll keep this world in its place once I've emerged as myself again, though?"

Turning away to the first aid kit, she shrugs. "Why would you destroy a world that was made for you? Where it's an easy system for someone like you to exploit and gain power?"

"I guess that's a good point."

Despina really is gorgeous. Athletic, covered head to toe in the taut muscles of a jungle cat, tanned and toned yet somehow so feminine. And that ass…ah, the kind fingers yearn to caress. When she turns back with the bandage in her hand, she catches me staring at her.

"Why'd you really do something as risky as bringing me back to your house, Despina?"

Sliding her hand around mine again, she applies the bandage with only the briefest of glances away from my face. When she looks back she's stuck there, as frozen before my gaze as the mouse before the cobra.

"I—I just wanted to help you."

"Is that it?" I look her carefully in the eye, smiling as her wrapping reaches its end. "Or did you want a chance to earn the favor of a demon lord?"

Her lower lip briefly vanishes into her mouth before springing back out to part in an anxious moue.

"We need your help," she says earnestly. "Like I said—without you, the planet serves no purpose on a metaphysical level. If you die, the human race is done. It evaporates. Worse, it's like it never existed at all."

Tapping my chin with my bandaged hand, I posit,

"Maybe there's another, more real human race somewhere. Another dimension, or something."

"What concern is that to my consciousness? Or yours, for that matter."

"If I'm as powerful as everybody is saying I am, maybe I could go elsewhere. If there's an elsewhere to go to, anyway…I mean, who knows?" I spread my hands. "Isn't the Devil supposed to be, you know, evil? Maybe I'll just choose to destroy the world myself someday."

"But what possible benefit could that hold for you? The angels want everything neat and tidy and under control. One unified energy acting in submission to God. The demons, on the other hand, get everything humans get and more when the world is existent. Power, success…sex."

Finished with my hand, Despina looks anxiously into my face and slides a hand over my chest. "Please. Don't forsake this world once your seals are broken. Fight not just for yourself, but for this world—for us—and we will do everything we can to help you in turn.

"The planet is sick, humanity is constantly at war. The human race isn't as good as it could be…but this is all we have, this place. All we've ever had, at least that we know of. Maybe to you this prison is some sort of simulation—but for me, this is where my parents are and where my ancestors were born. It's where my grandparents fell in love and then learned to hate each other. It's where I have a sister I barely see anymore. It's where I'd like to raise a child of my own someday."

Her eyes shimmer with glassy tears.

"Please," she whispers. "Please, Legion—as your true self wakes up, don't let it put *you* to sleep."

Lately I'm wondering if it isn't already too late for that. Lately I'm wondering if I've ever been awake at all.

"Lately," I tell her, "I'm wondering if Vic Legion even exists."

One single gem of a tear squeezes from the outer corner of her right eye.

We exchange a long look, the familiar mounting of tension—the silent understanding of mutual sexual desire.

Despina leans in to kiss me, her warm lips lightly parted and her eyelids fluttering closed.

While our mouths and lips entangle, so do our limbs, our noses, our bodies. Stumbling back, she draws me by the shirt to the bed of the adjoining room. In our walk through it earlier I remember thinking it was very austere; now, as she pushes me down upon its golden sheets, it had might as well be as empty as the void of my nest on the night I discovered the truth about myself.

"You should let me thank you for saving my life today," I tell her, glad my hands aren't so immobilized that I can't unbutton her jeans. After drawing them down to reveal her lacy panties with a sigh, I lay back upon her bed and tell her, "I can't use my hands, though."

She gets the message. Bending to kiss me while she wriggles out of her jeans and underwear, Despina next straightens up and slides her blouse up over her head. My cock twitches and I exclaim in delight to see her brown nipples are pierced. While she straddles my head and slowly lowers her beautiful copper pussy over my lips, I discover her clitoral hood is still unpierced, and that she is absolutely beautiful, and that the taste of her is as fine as a feminine wine.

"Oh! Fuck!" Despina gasps as soon as my flickering tongue makes contact with her flesh. Her hands raise to her breasts to cup and massage them while she rubs her vulva back and forth against my mouth, her pussy wetter by the second. "*Si,* please, *si,* oh, Legion—fuck, you're really good—"

And only getting better with all the practice I'm enjoying these days. While my tongue encourages the nervous flow of her arousal to rise from a trickle to a flood, the heady aroma of her body leaves me drunk with lust. That big, wonderful ass is right above me: I reach up to stroke and squeeze it while, with a moan, she leans down to liberate me from my trousers. As my cock springs out, I swear I feel her get even wetter.

"Oh, Legion…" Trailing her fingertips reverently over the shaft, then down to the balls she tenderly strokes while I sigh, Despina draws her hair back from her face with her free hand. Still grinding against my mouth, she bends down and carefully plants a few soft kisses along its twitching surface. As my tongue strains up into her valley, her moaning mouth slips around my cock.

Ah, man…demon blowjobs are nice, but there's something so refreshing, so natural, about a human woman's mouth—especially when she's just a little naïve in her approach. Not a virgin, but not exactly a porn star. There's a sweet spot in there where enthusiasm makes up for lack of experience, and that's where Despina is. She can't deepthroat, but she does her best, and I can tell by the long, loving strokes of her hand and the way her pussy flows with desire that she genuinely enjoys exploring my anatomy. Her soft tongue swirls persistently around the head, then works futilely against as much of the shaft as she can take into her mouth. The rest is covered by her diligent hands, the low vibrations of her moans inspiring me to work my tongue a little faster all the time.

It's when my hand lifts to lay a playful spank that she really cries out, though. Hurts my palm through the bandage, but it's damn worth it.

"Oh yeah?" My words are muffled against her flesh, but she can surely feel my grin. There's nothing quite like figuring out what really turns a woman on. I spank her again, harder, the flesh of her ass so ample I don't even have to aim to land a good one. While her pussy quivers, she cries out, lifting her head from my dick and substituting her hand.

"Oh, *Papi! Si*, yes, oh, fuck—yes—" The word catches in her throat with the next swat. While my tongue darts into her, she whimpers and writhes against my jaw. "Spank me, yes, oh, fuck—"

No need to tell me twice, although I wouldn't object to hearing her beg for a nice, long time. While just barely fucking her with the tip of my tongue I lay a barrage of sharp swats, each crueler than the last. Her reactions alone have me straining harder than ever in her hand, and as I spank her with one hand, I let the other pet her ass and graze the taut pucker between her cheeks like it's by accident. When it makes her moan, I tease her asshole with the tip of my finger. She cums in a second with that little addition…good to know.

"Ah! Oh, fuck—Legion! Oh, ah—"

While her trembling body collapses beside me, the orgasm annihilating her sense of balance or her desire to hold herself up, I laugh and bend over her to kiss the ridge of her ear. She whispers something and I have to ask her to repeat herself because it's so mumbled.

"Please fuck me," she whispers, whining a little, reaching back to tug my cock. "Please, Legion, oh, fuck—"

My prick twitches in her talented hand. She looks irresistible, her copper body splayed upon the sheets, and I want to bend her over the edge of the bed for hours—her pussy, displayed and dripping, wants it, too.

But I'm feeling cruel these days. I find I like it when

women beg for me. And, well…if I'm going to be a demon lord, I'd ought to play the part.

"You want me to fuck you, huh?" I tug one of her pierced nipples, rolling it between my fingers to make her moan. "I don't know…I have a gorgeous succubus fuck-slave begging for my cock at home. I could just go fuck her…use her however I want."

"Oh, please! Use *me*, Legion. Please, oh, fuck, I want to be owned by you—I want you to mark me as yours, please!"

While I twitch in her hand, I chuckle and bend down to brush my nose against hers. "Please, what?"

"Please, sir! Please, Master! Please—let me be your slave, Master!"

Kissing her gasping mouth, my tongue sliding in against hers to give her a taste of herself, I turn her body so she lies on her stomach and stuff a few pillows under her hips. With her gorgeous ass presented in the air and her legs akimbo, Despina moans in something close to embarrassment. The curve of her spine as she turns herself to look at me is enough to knock me out.

"What a hot body my new slave has," I tell her, running my fingers down the spread labia that positively drool for me. "You want your Master's cock, do you?"

"Yes, sir! Oh, please…please, I want your big, bare cock—I want you to fill me up with your cum so I can feel it dripping out of me after you're gone."

My bandaged hands roving over her ass, I wish to myself that I could feel her properly…but one part of me can feel her unencumbered, anyway. "All right," I tell her, the head of my dick pressing against her and making her moan right away, "since you were such a good girl and saved your master today, I'll give you a special treat…a nice, extra-hard fucking. Is this what you want?"

As I slowly push into her, she moans with high desperation and nods eagerly. "Yes," begs Despina, looking over her shoulder with one hand tangled in her own hair. "Yes, yes, please—oh! Master!"

After an inch or two, I can't resist anymore and ram myself home deep in her pussy. While we groan together, I spread her ass cheeks with my thumbs and admire that quivering hole. "You're a dirty little slut, aren't you, Despina? An athlete, a revolutionary, a hell of a fighter I'm sure…but underneath it all, you just want your master to treat you like a horny little bitch."

"Oh, fuck, please, yes—uh! Yes, sir, oh, fuck, I've wanted to meet you for so long…and then, when I saw your vessel for the first time, oh, I found myself wondering what it would be like if you fucked me—"

"How is it?"

"So good! So fucking good, oh, Master—oh, Master, Master, yes, please, fuck your human slave!"

Groaning, I pound her as hard and as fast as I want, my thumb pressing against her asshole to make her scream with ecstasy. "You love it when Master touches you there, huh, slave?"

"Yes! Oh, yes, please, touch me anywhere—"

Her eyes meet mine from where she stares over her shoulder. I push my thumb just inside her rectum and she gasps, moans, grips around my cock, then is suddenly overcome with an orgasm that furrows her brow and seems almost to hurt her.

"Oh, sir," she screams, "oh, Master! Oh yes, yes, yes, yes! Let me be your slave for eternity, Master! Fuck me like this forever!"

The screaming of her orgasm comes to a background of flesh slapping on flesh. As I bend to kiss her cheek and ear she shudders and moans. My name drifts from her mouth, the soft, "Legion," making me twitch in her. I'm near the edge—but I have a character to play.

"Master," I correct her, lifting my hand away from her ass and bringing it down in a sharp spank.

Despina gasps, whining with pleasure—especially as the next set of spanks lands along with my hard strokes into her. I fuck her mercilessly while, each swat, she screams for more and more. My hand aches through the bandage, but it doesn't matter. Nothing matters. The only thing that matters is getting to the finish line—alleviating the agonizing height of pleasure in an orgasm that arrives like a suckerpunch. My body tenses in and against hers, and while she moans I reach around her hip to toy with her clitoris. As the explosion of my pleasure releases a few spurts of cum deep in her desperate pussy, I massage her to a rapid third orgasm that makes her scream with pleasure.

"Yes, please," she begs, sweetening my orgasm with her continued desire. "Yes, Master! Oh, yes, give me all that cum, please, sir, oh, I need it, yes, I need it—"

Well, hell…not like I'm using it for anything.

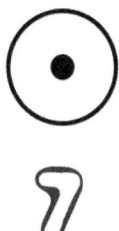

AFTER A SHOWER and a change of wound dressings, Despina and I intend only to rest but drop into a hefty sleep. The morning has been so draining that, when I awaken in Despina's bed mid-afternoon, I struggle to piece together the chain of events that's landed me there.

When I remember, at the very least, the vigorous and highly fun events that have taken place in this bedroom, I stir fully from my sleep and lift my head to look for Despina.

Nowhere to be found.

Sitting up, I rub my eyes with the unbandaged tips of my fingers and push a few locks of hair back upon my head. The alarm clock by the bed declares it's 2:43, which would explain why I'm famished, and why I feel like I've been dead. Beside the alarm clock is a note.

"Master"—

Things to do.
If you need me someday
and I'm not around,
call me.

Love,

Despina

The note ends with her phone number and smells like her patchouli-laden body. I tuck it into my pocket once I've put the number into my phone and gotten my clothes back on.

Walking back through the house, I take stock of the rooms and find it comes off as somehow false. Like a model home in a housing development, arranged to attract buyers but providing little to no utility. At least the apple I take from the kitchen counter is real. I take a few bites of the juicy red fruit while using my other hand to fiddle with my phone. First I call the garage to see if the car is ready—no such luck, tomorrow morning for sure—and then, realizing I don't know the address of the place, I have to use my phone to look up the street name and step outside to take a gander at the number.

Then I call a taxi cab, because Uber and other ride-sharing services are beneath me. I'd rather take a city bus than make forced conversation with a driver thirsty for a rating on some app.

Told you I've always been like this.

At home, the place quiet without Baphomet trying to get my dick out of my pants, I take a little time to think about all of this. Angels at Helcom; people, maybe the same angels, assailing me in the streets; all this power, and what it could do. The real fear in Despina's eyes during little moments of our conversation, when the subject was the end of this world.

She gave me some interesting food for thought. Interesting most especially because it took a human's argument to alleviate any moral hesitance I felt about what was evidently my true nature. Not only had she, as an outsider, confirmed that I was what the succubus and the nest and all the other wild goings-on told me I was… she had also informed me that whatever sin had gotten me put here had also created this world, or at the very least created a need and context for the world.

There's a sense of such fearful respect pervading my interactions with Despina. Even during our sex she had been in awe of me, eager to submit—and though her quotation marks around *Master* in that note make it a little wry, we all from time to time use sarcasm to say in jest what we'd like to say in earnest. I press the note to my lips while thinking of her in a new study I've discovered around the corner from Beatrix's bedroom, the high back of the leather chair there a fine place to rest my head and contemplate until my servant finds me.

"There you are, Master—*Master!*"

Gasping, Baphomet rushes in and catches one of my bandaged hands in hers. "What happened?"

"It's been a long day."

While I tell her about the assault, she investigates the bandage and slowly unwinds it from around my hand. Frowning, the succubus looks up at me from the shadows of her horns, then studies the scrapes across my palm.

"I told you that you must be careful," she says, shaking her head, then poising her hand an inch above mine. "Please hold still, sir."

A warm, vaguely itchy sensation crawls across my hand, as though a tarantula walks from my fingers to my wrist. While a red light glows between her hand and mine, my flesh knits before my astonished eyes. Could I have done this with manifestation magic, I wonder?

"I didn't know you had this ability."

"We demons can do many things, Master—more things when we are in our nests, and more still when we are well-fed." With a noise like a purr, her tail lashes. Baphomet gazes up at me in adoration. "You keep me very nearly sated, Master."

"I'm glad to hear it…our mystery girl Despina should meet you sometime. What do you know about this group that she's in?"

Baphomet shakes her head. "Such organizations are not my area of expertise. We will have to consult with Gretchen when we're able to connect with her—she is one of your servants, sir, one of my sisters. She is extremely well-versed in human history and anthropological matters, as she has walked the Earth in many guises for many centuries."

"Where can she be found?"

"I'm not sure. She will be somewhere near you, but we four split ways when the world was made so as to find you while posing minimal risk to ourselves. We are drawn naturally to your energy, so will all find you in time…and, as all our energies come together, we will act as a sort of beacon. Not just for other demons, but for angels, too."

Frowning, sliding into my lap, Baphomet trails her crimson fingernail down my cheek and whimpers sweetly.

"I'm worried about you, Master. How can I protect you when I'm hunting for angels through the celestial haze at Helcom?"

"I can take care of myself," I tell her, stroking her thigh through the diamond gaps of her fishnet stocking. While she moans, goosebumps rising over her bare shoulder, I kiss the edge of her mouth and soon earn a long, desirous one in return. "You're so sensitive, Baphomet…I really do barely have to touch you to get you wound up."

While my hand slides between her slightly splayed legs to test this theory, she moans again and runs her fingers through my hair. "I love it when you touch me, sir…oh, I love it when you come home from fucking other women…how was it?"

As I tease her through her thong and marvel to feel her already soaking through the silk, I tell her, "Despina was very hot…she liked to call me 'Master.'"

"Another slave for you! Oh, goodie, Master—and your first human slave in this form…oh!"

With my healed hands, I push aside her g-string and admire the drenched pussy desperate for my attention beneath. As I humor her by sliding a finger in, I tell Baphomet, "She had a nice, tight cunt…ah, and she got so fucking wet after a good spanking."

"Mm, oh, I love getting spanked…and spanking humans…oh!"

Unable to resist, I slide my finger back out and lift my hand to land a sharp smack on her vulva. Squealing with pleasure, the demoness splays her legs and runs her hands up over her breasts.

"Oh! Sir, yes, please, sir, spank my pussy—oh, nice and hard, that's it, that's it…"

I've never seen a woman as horny, pun fully intended, as this demoness. Baphomet pants like a bitch in heat, moaning and writhing in my lap while I tease her. "You really do like this, huh? I'll be sure to punish you all the time, Baphomet…where was I? Oh, yeah…Despina loved having her asshole touched. You should watch me fuck her in the ass when I finally do it."

"Fuck, yes, I'd love that, oh, yes, sir, yes—"

Reaching down to tug at the flesh of her vulva and expose her sensitive valley to my swats all the more, Baphomet thrashes in my lap and stares eagerly up at me. "I want to watch you fuck all kinds of women," she says while I slide my fingers into her. "Oh, fuck, please, yes, sir—let me watch you fuck Despina, Master, please!"

She's so dripping wet I can't stand it. These women! It's impossible for a man to have time to think when all these gorgeous, thirsty women around are begging for attention. Not that I'm complaining…

"If you're a very good girl," I tell her, sliding my finger from her flooded cunt and nudging her out of my lap, "I'll even let you help."

"Please, sir! Yes, please, oh, I want to make Despina cum with you…ah! Master!"

Moaning with delight to see me take my cock out, the demoness lays back over the arm of the chair with her pussy on the offer. Soon I'm wrapped in her wonderful legs, my cock sliding effortlessly into the drenched vacuum of her tight channel. As I groan and fuck her, I tell her, "Be sure to scream nice and loud so Melody can hear you, baby…"

"Hn! Please! Yes, sir, oh, yes, sir! Give me your big, hard cock, fuck, oh! Pound me so rough, oh, I need it hard, make it hurt, please, sir—ah!"

While I hammer her as deep and hard as I can, my abdomen slapping against her clit to sweeten her pleasure each stroke, she moans and frees her breasts. "Despina's got gorgeous tits, pierced." I pinch one of her nipples and she bucks wildly against me, her mouth open in shock at the intensity of the pleasure. "And oh, she begged for my cock like a champion…my cum, too."

"Oh! Oh, Master, did you already cum in your new slave?"

"I sure did, baby, ah—buried a load nice and deep in her hot little pussy so she knows she's mine."

"Ah! Oh, yes, oh, fuck, sir, what a lucky slave she is! Oh, Master, will you please cum in me, too? I love to feel your semen dripping out of me all the time…mm, I was enjoying it at work all day today…I would have enjoyed it even more if I had known you were off fucking some new human slave…"

"Well, maybe next time I'll send you a video."

She giggles, running her hands over her breasts and rolling her stiff nipples between her fingers. "I'd love that, Master…oh, yes, please, I'd love that…"

After we've reached our inevitable conclusions, I come to draped in the armchair with the demoness content in my arms. She smiles to see me stir from the post-coital coma into which she's sent me, her fingers trailing over my chest and up along my jaw.

"Aren't you hungry by now, Master? Don't forget to eat."

"I won't," I tell her, adding as she gets up, "oh—by the way, I've got to pick my car up from the garage tomorrow morning. Would you be able to give me a ride?"

But Baphomet only laughs at me.

"Silly Master! I don't have a car…I'm a demon! I just turn invisible and fly everywhere."

Ah, yes. Why wasn't I thinking?

"Can I manifest a car?"

"How are you going to get it down the elevator?"

With a roll of my eyes, I feel momentary remorse for not picking a first floor apartment, or just biting the bullet and renting a house…but, were that the case, I wouldn't have Melody for a neighbor.

Hey. Now there's an idea.

The next morning, after calling work to tell them I'll be in a bit late, I stop by Melody's apartment. Following a delay of about forty-five seconds, an amount just long enough for me to worry that she's not even up, the door cracks. It opens wider with her gasp.

"Good morning, neighbor," she says in a playful, pleasant way, her lilac tinted hair down for the first time I've seen and looking so incredibly beautiful around her pale face that she somehow resembles a porcelain doll— or maybe, better still, a ghost. Smiling wide, blushing to see me, she draws her light pink robe more tightly closed with one hand. She holds it shut while staring with affection into my eyes. "You're by early today."

"I'm just a bum here to beg for a favor," I say. "Will you save me a taxi ride and give me a lift near downtown? I've got to pick up my car from a garage."

"Oh!" A few strands of hair sliding down her shoulder to hang against her collarbone, Melody looks at me in surprise and seems almost pleased to be asked such a thing. She smiles again, a little wider now. "Of course! Do you have a minute for me to finish my coffee and get dressed?"

"No, you have to drive me naked…sure, there's time." While she laughs, the tips of her ears just poking through the streams of hair and glowing red already, I help myself to a seat in the corner of her couch. "I called work and told them I'd be a little late…I'm not sure the garage will even be open for another hour or two."

"In that case, do you want some coffee?"

Soon she's beside me, the hint of knee poking through her robe sufficient to make me understand why Edwardian men went crazy for a well-turned ankle. When a woman who's so shy and reserved gives even a hint of what lays beneath, the mind can't help but wander. I want to touch her right away but don't want to make her feel like I'm getting too handsy, so I keep focused on the coffee mug and maintain eye contact whenever possible.

"This is a really nice surprise…I feel like I've been thinking about you since you left my apartment the other day."

"Oh yeah? Thinking what?"

Getting that shy look again, Melody sips her brew and smiles mysteriously. "I'm just looking forward to Monday, is all…oh, but I didn't ask. What happened to your car?"

"Mm? Oh, nothing…just a car chase." She laughs. I smile, humoring her in what she thinks is a joke before I go on to say truthfully, "I got impatient and pulled a stupid u-turn over a median. Cacti were involved. It was all bad news."

Hissing sympathetically, she crosses her legs, readjusts her robe and tells me, "That sounds like a lesson learned."

"It sure was." The lesson is don't trust angels—and be prepared at all times for one to show up from around a corner. "I met an interesting person yesterday, though."

"Oh?"

"Yeah…this chick gave me a ride…she was very hot."

This sentence alone is enough to enrich the depth of the scarlet upon my neighbor's face. "O—oh, really?"

"She sure was. Does that make you jealous, Melody?"

"No! Well—maybe yes, a little. But—I don't know."

Unable to articulate her thoughts, she utters a nervous laugh and looks away from my face. "Maybe feeling jealous gets me excited."

Now I dare to touch her; just to push a few strands of hair behind her ear and caress my thumb along the temple of her forehead while she gasps.

"Well…you don't need to be jealous, Melody, trust me. You're two entirely different types of women, I think. Though I like the thought of you getting all wet with jealousy."

Though she laughs slightly, mostly she gazes at me with heavy eyes and lips that hover, parted in faint hope for a kiss. Searching her flushed face, I tell her, "Beatrix's pussy was so wet yesterday when I was telling her about this woman, this Despina…I'm sure yours gets that way, too, huh?"

"Oh—uh, I don't, uh—"

"Did you listen last night, by the way? Have you gotten lots of practice in at touching yourself?"

Biting her lip, Melody nods after only the slightest delay. "I like listening to you—fuck her." The word seems almost hard to get out. As I set aside my coffee mug, she watches my face with dreamy eyes. "I was so excited the other day, when you left me without doing anything and then made her scream. How did you fuck her?"

"Right against the wall," I tell Melody, glancing down at her robe. "The break wall of the kitchen…she's a desperate slut. I barely have to walk into a room and she's wet for me. How about you, Melody?"

With a gentle hand, I slowly invade the folds of her robe to elicit a gasp and a glance down—but no argument. As my fingers brush one slightly hard nipple to make it stand at further attention, she moans in a way so sweet my dick strains in my trousers. "Are you wet for me right now, Melody?"

"Oh—I—I—"

"Tell me the truth, now," I tell her, tugging gently on her nipple.

Moaning, red-faced, Melody nods.

"Yes! Yes, oh, Vic...I'm very wet right now."

I release her nipple and withdraw my hand. "Show it to me."

Melody gasps as though scandalized, but the breathiness of it indicates the pleasure she takes in the idea. "Wh—just like that? Here? Now?"

"Don't be shy, Melody...you let me see it last time. Just let me look."

Biting her lip, my neighbor look down at herself. I think for a second she's going to go shy on me and refuse, but instead my blood thrills. She unties the front of the robe, her eyes locked on mine until she shrugs the plush fabric from her shoulders and lets me see every inch of her.

God damn, Melody is beautiful. There is something young and fresh about her body, maybe because she's more svelte than the busty demoness or athletic Latina ladies I've been consorting with of late. Instead, Melody is delicate but soft, her body a painting of creamy whites and floral pinks and, yes, that irresistible hint of silvery hair crowning the dew-soaked flower of her pussy. I moan as she turns toward me and spreads her legs to present herself, her labia drooping apart to permit the lucky lights to catch the shimmer of her folds.

"What a cute little virgin pussy," I tell her with a sigh. "Are you going to let me fuck it in front of Beatrix on Monday?"

Whimpering sweetly, Melody nods and slides closer to me. I reach over and draw her into my lap, her noise of surprise making me all the harder. While her bare ass settles down against the tent in my pants, I run my hands up and down her body—her breasts, her neck, her back, ass, thighs. I touch her everywhere but her pussy, left available by her spread legs.

"Yes," whispers my neighbor while I tease her writhing body. "Oh, yes! Legion, please, I want you to fuck me so badly…I want to be seen with your dick in me, I want to see someone getting off to the idea of your dick being in me…oh, Legion, Legon!"

I can't stand it anymore. My finger trails over her labia and that alone has her nearly screaming with ecstasy. As I tickle around her clitoris, she whines and rocks against my cock. "Mm! Oh, Legion—I want to feel what it's like. I want to see it."

Gasping, turning to clutch me by the shirt, my allegedly innocent neighbor bites her lip and begs, "*May I see it?*"

Exhaling, I slide my hand away from her and let her turn around in my lap. While she kneels over me, I free myself from my trousers.

Melody moans with lust, astonished, her eyes bright with desire and fear alike.

"Oh, Legion! It's so *big*. How will it fit?"

"We just have to get this beautiful pussy of yours nice and wet, first." I touch her gorgeous labia while she kneels there, admiring my cock between us. On the contact she gasps, then moans and leans into my fingertips. As I resume steadily teasing her clit, she looks shyly up at me, then down at my twitching prick.

Uncertainly, Melody trails her fingers over the head of my cock. I groan, and soon her unsure caress turns into more avid fondling. As she gently tugs the head, she looks me in the eyes and whispers, "Does that feel good?"

"That feels so good, baby…oh, so good…hah, ah, and feeling how wet your pussy is just makes it better. Ah—"

"Oh…" With a sad, girlish whimper, she bites her lip and says softly, "I want to feel you inside of me, but I'm so nervous."

"Don't be nervous…we can take all the time we need, Melody, and whenever you're ready, I promise I'll be gentle. Unless you don't want me to be, of course."

Looking tempted but still uncertain, Melody looks up into my face and lowers herself toward my dick. Guiding my glans with that experimental hand, she pleasures herself with my anatomy and moans to find I watch her at it. Her pussy drips all over my straining length, and, sighing, I let myself be washed away in the bliss of her teasing.

"It feels so hot! And so hard…but the skin is so smooth…hm—" She whimpers as she lets my cock push up against the drenched entrance of her channel. While her quim flutters around me and I groan, she whines softly, "Oh, Legion—I want to feel you in me, I want that so much, ah—I don't have any condoms, though—"

"I've had a vasectomy," I assure her, leaning to brush my lips over hers. "It's all right."

"Really? Really? Oh—oh—Legion, I *really* want you—"

"Do you want to show me to your bedroom? Come on…let's get comfortable."

We're there in a flash. Poised on the edge of her four-post bed, naked and beautiful and flushed with desire, Melody watches me undress and perks when I'm naked. "You're so beautiful," she whispers, her eyes foggy with desire.

"I could say the same." My hand fits to the back of her head and, while kissing her, I urge her back upon the soft mattress. She strokes my chest and neck and scalp until I draw back to see her displayed beneath me; then her hands fall away and one shyly rests upon her cheek while the other hides a breast. This beautiful hand, I lift away and hold.

I keep holding it as, between her legs, I fit myself against her and take her virginity with a firm but gentle push.

I expected her to find it painful, and her eyes do widen, but from the first second she gasps in bliss. Soon her wide eyes flutter instead, and as I take to slowly working myself in and out of her impeccably tight body, Melody slides her arms around my neck and gazes into my face. Her breath comes in soft moans every stroke I make up into her, and while my length bumps her g-spot she drenches me with her arousal.

"Legion! Oh, Legion, Legion, you feel so wonderful! Oh—I can't believe you fit inside me, how nice, oh, Legion—"

Though I love to be rough with a woman who wants it, there's something to be said for tender lovemaking with somebody like Melody. She positively trembles with years of unexpressed libido, enraptured by my face while I cradle her close to my body. Her legs wrap around me and I fit a hand to her rear, not to increase my own pleasure by experiencing her body but to embrace her close to me— to fit her to me as tightly as a woman can fit to a man. Soon our mouths are connected, and, coiled around one another like a pair of snakes, our bodies writhe at a pace dictated by the desperation of her sweet little moans. I don't even need to touch her beyond romantic caresses of her limbs: our fit truly is perfect, and it isn't long before I catch a note in her voice that makes me fuck her a little harder than I yet have.

"Legion!" My name rises from her in a kind of surprise. While whimpering, she takes my pounding like a champion and seems almost shocked as I make her cum. "Legion—oh! Oh! Oh, God—"

I somehow manage to avoid laughing at the world's most common sexual expression, which certainly doesn't belong in any bedroom of mine anymore. But, of course, this is Melody's bedroom…her innocent, old-fashioned bedroom, which my mere presence violates.

She doesn't seem to care, though. As she cums, she presses her hand to my cheek and arches up to kiss me. The sweetness of her kiss and the bold explorations of her flickering tongue are sufficient to make me spill in her with a few more well-aimed thrusts. As I groan against her mouth, she whines with delight and kisses me all the more savagely.

Soon, panting, we separate and gaze adoringly at one another.

"There," I say, pushing a few strands of hair from Melody's soft eyes. "Still nervous?"

She laughs.

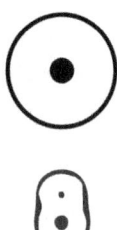

MELODY CURLS IN my arms and murmurs with me for half an hour after we've finished, her body aglow with rapture and a certain hint of pride in her face. Have I taken a woman's virginity before? I'm not so sure that I have, or that it even really matters to me…but it certainly seems to matter to her. Looking like the cat that got the canary, Melody gets up after she's recovered some of her stamina and asks, "Did you have time for breakfast?"

After an incredible meal of homemade pancakes, bacon and eggs, Melody showers, dresses, and drives me to the garage. With neighbors like this, who needs demon slaves? Not that the two are mutually exclusive.

"I'll see you on Monday," she says with a coy smile as I kiss her cheek. "Or maybe before."

Then, when she's driven off, I head into the garage to assess the monetary damage.

Not as bad as I thought, though I have to admit my eyes glaze over while the guy explains the problem to me. I'm just not a car man…or car demon, I guess.

There really are two 'me's, I've been thinking since my encounter with Despina. There's this me, the temporal me. Then there's this demonic me, this phantom floating above me. The cause of all this trouble for myself and everyone around me…and the person whose existence is maintaining the world.

How different are these two states? Is there any clear third state where the two aspects could exist in harmony, or can that only be described by a observing total timeline of my life?

I suppose everybody has these questions as they start to become the adult they were always destined to be. After all…there's being an adult, and then there's *becoming* an adult. It doesn't happen overnight. I'm thirty now, and I've only recently stopped thinking of myself as a seventeen-year-old for some reason. Sometimes the shift is so gradual you don't even notice it, this process of maturation.

And then sometimes it's thrust upon you by extraordinary circumstances.

At work, the office is unusually chatty. Mike is standing outside of his cubicle for once, sipping coffee and leaning in on the person across the row from us. When he sees me, he waves good-bye to them and greets me with a grin.

"Glad to see you! When Gabe called in again today I was starting to worry there was a genuine bug going around."

I laugh a little, slinging down my jacket and telling

him, "Nah, I just got caught up in something yesterday… car trouble. Easier to take off than scramble in."

"I feel that."

"So he called in yesterday, too?"

"Sure did. I'm sure he'll be back tomorrow, though… no way will he miss the department pool tournament. You want to smoke with me before you start?"

Out on the patio, Mike shoots the shit with me about a fantasy series we're both reading (generally he gives me pulp fiction, while I give him horror) and is just asking, "So what's the deal with these black cigarettes," when the door opens.

Beatrix steps into the sunlight, squinting past the smokers clustered here and there on a slow work day with the manager out of the office. While I nod at her, she trots over and asks, "Can I bum a light?"

All eyes are on her as I produce a lighter for her use. With a sensual parting of her ruby lips against white teeth and a glance that has me eager to get home after work, she takes the lighter in her fingers and says, "Thank you…now, can I bum a smoke?"

Laughing, I shake out the pack and let her pick one while saying, "Have I introduced myself yet?"

"I don't think so. I'm Beatrix." While she shakes my hand and the mildly distracted conversations pick up their patter when other engineers see they've missed their shot with Beatrix for this smoke break, Mike looks curiously at me. I ignore him and introduce myself, then Mike. His face reddens to shake her hand but she looks about as interested in him—or anybody else, for that matter—as most people would be in a tree or a chair.

"Nice to officially meet you, Mike," she says with a professional smile. Then, lighting the cigarette and trading me back the lighter, she says, "I don't mean to interrupt you gentlemen. What were you talking about?"

Both staring at the 'o' of her perfect lips on her exhalation of clove-scented smoke, Mike and I exchange a glance.

"Fantasy," we say in time, prompting a cheeky little smile from the demoness.

After work, with Frank quietly cleaning the bar, Mike and I sit together in front of a couple of beers. He marvels over the incident during our smoke break: I'm laughing while he shakes his head.

"It's crazy to me," says my friend. "I just can't do it."

"Sure you can!"

"No, I can't. I just can't pick up on women."

"You have to stop thinking about it like that. You're just talking to them! Feeling them out. Metaphorically, I mean, of course."

"But what if I come off creepy or weird?"

"You won't."

"I don't know, Vic…I can really put my foot in my mouth when I'm nervous. And women make me *nervous.*"

"Women don't make you nervous," I tell him, lifting my beer to my lips, "*boobs* make you nervous. Potential rejection makes you nervous. Women are just people."

"But—they have different priorities!"

"Maybe once upon a time they did, or were convinced they did…but I think everybody's pretty much on the same page these days. It's just a matter of meeting the right person who wants to have sex. Very simple. You're letting your desire to perform well cloud the important stuff. 'Picking up on women,' as you called it, is *supposed* to be fun—for everybody. It's two hot adults coming together and saying, "You're hot, I'm hot, I like sex, you like sex, we're both free tonight, let's go hang out.""

"But what if they don't think I'm hot?"

"If you think you're hot, they'll think you're hot…and if you don't think you're hot, learn how to style yourself and start lifting weights or something. Attractiveness is a matter of attitude and presentation, not of body or even intelligence. Think of how many terrible movies had great trailers or posters."

Sighing, he shakes his head. "I just can't deal with rejection, though."

"Ah, come on. Rejection happens all the time in life. What's the worst that's going to happen? Somebody will insult you or belittle you. I've had it happen to me. That's just part of life, you know? Rejection, assholes—these things are just part of the natural order, my friend. You've got to hold your head up and remember that you're not 'picking up on a woman' just to pick up on a woman… you're picking up on a woman to have fun and make a friend who might be more than a friend. Just remember: They're people who just happen to *have* boobs, not boobs who happen to have a person guarding access to them."

Frank laughs without looking up from the glass he polishes. While I grin over at him, Mike laughs along just a little.

"Yeah," he says weakly, "I guess that's true. I just get so in my own head all the time, you know?"

"We've all been there, my guy. Let me get your drink."

He pauses mid-grab for his wallet, asking, "Really?"

One way or another I just don't think I'm going to worry about money for much longer in my life…and, at any rate, I've always been a bit of a spendthrift. Easy come, easy go. "Sure, my treat. I'll be here a few minutes more I think, anyway."

"All right! I'll get you back tomorrow…catch you later. Have a good night, Frank!"

The old man waves, setting the final polished glass

down as Mike makes his exit. When the door has fully shut, Frank shakes his head and chuckles. "You've got the patience of a saint, Vic."

"That means something, coming from you. If I had to listen all day to conversations like the one we just had, I think I'd lose my mind."

"It's not so bad. Certainly helps the work fly by...I don't have to watch the cable at all." He jerks his thumb at the old television hanging over the bar before taking the twenty I slide to him. "Get you another?"

"Nah, but keep the change."

"Bless you, son...say, uh"—Frank glances up from his till as he slaps the little lever down over the twenty— "whatever happened with that girl you were with on Monday?"

"Oh—the blonde, Beatrix?" I laugh a little at his question and shake my head. Lifting my beer to my lips, I leave it at, "I think she's doomed to be a fixture of my life for the foreseeable future."

"Mmhm."

Frank is the kind of guy who only lets you have his advice when you ask for it...and when you ask for it, he really lets you have it. Setting my beer down on the bar as he turns away to busy himself with something else, I say, "You have thoughts on that?"

"Oh, well, it's none of my business. It's just—" He pauses whatever he was about to do and sighs in a weighty way, resting the heels of both his palms against the bar. "You know, Vic, when you're in my business you get a certain sense for people. That girl, she seemed like trouble to me."

"She's trouble, all right."

Looking at me in a cockeyed way now, Frank says, "There's trouble that adds a little cinnamon, and then there's trouble that'll land a man in the electric chair."

"It's lethal injection now, Frank."

"All I'm telling you is to be careful," he continues, slapping the back of my free hand with his stained bar rag. While I scoff and rub the spot like a remonstrated kid, he goes on with a thematically appropriate wag of his finger. "And don't say I didn't warn you. You seemed to be having your share of problems with her on Monday, you know...I see you storm out and drive off, and the next thing I know this chick sprints out of my bar like her ass is on fire."

She had to if she was going to fly to my apartment before I showed up.

"I appreciate your concern," I tell him honestly. "I do. And I'll take it under advisement."

"Doesn't this lady work with you? You need to be doubly careful."

"I will."

"Mmhm," says the bartender again, assessing the container of limes and deciding to cut a few more. "Yeah, we'll just see about that."

Though I stew for a few seconds and contemplate defending myself a bit more on the subject, synchronicity saves the day. My cell phone rings and I read its screen with a sudden sting of guilt.

MOM

Ugh. I knew I've been forgetting something.

"Mom," I say quickly as I pick up the phone, "shit, sorry I forgot to call you back."

"Oh, dear, it's fine," she responds in a put-upon voice that's only half faked. "I'm only the person who gave birth to you, that's all...no big deal."

A weird series of thoughts flashes through my head. Is she, really? In the physical sense, I suppose…but, looking at it that way, she's more like the portal I first used to enter this world.

How strange. Am I losing my mind?

"I know, I need to treat you better. I'm sorry."

"Well, you've got an opportunity, although it's probably too late. I was wondering if you felt like taking the day off on Friday and giving your old Mom a ride up to the Gem and Mineral show!"

Just that sentence is enough to make me regret picking up the phone, as if her guilt trip hadn't been sufficient already. My mind's eye filling with post-traumatic flashbacks of row after row of vendors selling poorly organized boxes of fancy colored rocks, I kick back the remainder of my beer glass and nod at Frank. "I don't know, Mom," I say, making my way out of the bar and back to my car. "It really is short notice, you're not kidding."

"Well it *wouldn't* have been short notice if you had picked up your phone on Monday, or called me back, or done anything other than ignore my calls until the last possible moment!"

"Sorry," I say, trying to mean it. "It's been a busy week. I really did think about calling you back sooner."

"Uh-huh."

"I did!"

"Well, it's all right. I can always just skip the show this year."

"Why don't I drive you on Sunday? I'm not doing anything then. Even Saturday morning, if you promise not to take all night."

"I'm a busy girl, Victor! Your mother has places to be." While I start the car and plug in the phone for

Bluetooth, she hears the change on the line and asks, "Are you driving?"

"No," I lie while backing out of my space. "But you're lucky if I do decide to take you, because my car just got out of the shop this morning."

"Oh, honey! What happened?"

"Part of the long week, I don't want to get into it." Repressing a deep sigh, I rub my thumb against the ridge of my brow while waiting for my turn to join the traffic on the street. Well…I guess Gabe wasn't there today, was he? He'll have enough to get caught up on tomorrow that he probably won't even think about yet another absence from me. So much for treating this week like my first week at the company…maybe next week.

"All right," I tell her while she cheers. "Because I feel bad about not returning your call, I'll take you to the show."

"Oh, yes! This'll be wonderful. It reminds me of when you were a little kid, ah, Vic. What a cutie you were." While I shake my head patiently at the tenderness in her voice, my mother continues, "Maybe we'll get lunch, sweetheart. It'll be fun, don't worry."

"It had its charms," I say, remembering rows of cool cow skulls carved with intricate designs and old swirling ammonites from the dawn of time. "I just have a work thing in the evening that I can't miss."

"It won't be a problem! We'll grab a bite, look around for an hour or two, then head on home."

Famous last words.

"All right. When should I pick you up?"

After a brief conversation, a time and a destination for lunch is decided. I hang up with a sigh, already exhausted by the idea of all this. What a week! Good thing I already called in on Wednesday…I can act like I had a relapse of some food sickness or virus or something.

At home, I log into my work e-mail to send a message to Gabe about missing tomorrow. When I do, a new message pops up—one from Raphael. I've nearly forgotten he exists.

Dear Vic,

It was good meeting you the other day. Hope you're giving some thought to coming up to the sales floor. Let me know soon, if you can. We're swamped!

Hope to hear from you,

Raphael

It's always something. After jotting a quick e-mail to Gabe and blaming my poor attendance on further car problems I hope will be resolved before the pool tournament, I consider responding to Raphael that I've got too much going on right now to take on a new job... but I don't. Before my hands hit the keyboard, they pause. When they finally land on the desk, it's only on the mouse. Only to close the browser and leave me staring at the generic wallpaper.

What am I doing with my life? I really wonder. If I'm going to dwell here as a demon lord to maintain the integrity of the world, I had damn well better be rewarding myself for it. Am I really going to just sit around in a cubicle the whole time? Staring at a gray fabric wall, feeling nothing until I can finally leave for the day without risking my job?

Nah...there has to be a better way to live.

Still, I decide to keep Raphael hanging. I look up

directions to the mineral show, then get up and manifest a bite to eat while standing in the kitchen. It just sort of feels weird for me to make a sandwich appear for myself anywhere else. Kind of depressing, too. Unstructured.

Manifestation is fascinating to me. The truth is that there's been so much going on—and even with my time off I've been working enough—that I haven't spent a lot of time in my apartment this week. What time I do spend, I'm usually being distracted by Baphomet. There haven't been many opportunities to experiment with my new power.

But it occurs to me that I really could do all sorts of things with it. For instance, you want to talk about gems and minerals? Maybe I can manifest a gem so gorgeous I could sell it at the show and make a mint. If I did, would it be a unique gem, or would its molecules just so happen to form an exact copy of another gem somewhere out there in the world?

Furthermore, if I will the manifestation of a brand-new type of gem, a novel stone never before perceived upon Earth, wouldn't that stone only be novel with respect to Earth's existing stones—and therefore, still just derivative?

I'm starting to understand why there's so much ire between demons and angels, or myself and the big G-D. Sort of annoying when everything you want to do has already been done. When every concept you could think has, by virtue of its thinkabilty, already been established on some indiscernible level of reality?

Such a thing was reassuring, though, in its way. That structure again. Without the aspects of the world that fill up all its little details, how could I even think these thoughts?

Still chewing the last bite of my sandwich, I dust

off my hands and sweep mine a few inches above the countertop. When my palm passes, a perfectly round stone sits upon the kitchen island. Its surface is so absolutely fuligin black, so voracious for light, that it exhibits no reflections—yet seems for all the world to possess a kind of sheen. My eye can find no purchase upon it, I discover, and however dedicatedly I try to look at it, I often end up looking only at its edges. Only at the place where the nothingness of its surface cuts a hole out of the counter.

Lips parted in wonder, I pluck the stone up between my thumb and forefinger, examine it in the light, and try to determine what kind of mineral it is.

The front door opens and I slide it into my pocket.

"Master," says Beatrix with a pleased sigh to see me. "What a long day it was at the office! I'm just about starved."

"Aren't you always?"

Her grin shifting to a sensual, predatory smile, the demoness twirls and dons her natural form. As her golden hair flows back from her horns, she says, "Only when I'm alone with you, sir."

"You make my dick so hard, Baphomet…get down on your hands and knees."

Moaning with delight, her tail quivering with anticipation, the succubus elegantly bends down and crawls to me, face flushed and lowered. When she's within grabbing distance, I clutch a handful of golden hair and make her moan by yanking her head back.

"I had somebody warn me against spending my time with such a crazy slut," I tell her, staring down into her moaning mouth and those red eyes hooded with lust. "But you wouldn't betray me, would you, slave?"

"Oh, Master, no, no! I would never—I'm your first

girl, your favorite. I would do anything for you, sir. Please, oh…"

Moaning, biting her lip, she slides her hands up my legs and rubs the front of my trousers. "I know all of this sounds extraordinary," she says, gazing earnestly up at me from where she kneels at my feet. "But I swear to you, sir, it's real…I'm telling you everything I know, and I'm doing everything I can for you. And, if you don't believe me…"

Her hand slides up to the buckle of my belt while her red eyes focus lustfully on mine.

"Maybe you should make sure I know my place."

"Get to your master's bedroom, slut," I tell her, releasing her with a shove in its direction.

At her giddy cry, I hide my smirk by going to wash my hands of any potential remaining sandwich debris. Then, taking my time, I check the lock on the front door, shut down the hall lights for the night, and step into the bedroom where my gorgeous demon slave already sits upon the bed, her hands behind her as she props herself up to see me. She has stripped off all her clothes—magicked them away in an instant, perhaps—and displays herself, clearly eager for my eye, with nothing more than her thong.

Wanting her to suffer, I look away from her quickly. Then, with the door shut behind me to permit her no escape, I unbuckle my belt and slide it free of my trousers.

"You're going to be sorry you're always prancing around in that skimpy little thong," I tell her, doubling the leather over and cracking it experimentally against my hand. Moaning, Baphomet runs her hands over her breasts.

"But I need to feel your eyes on me all the time, Master."

"I know you do, you little attention whore…"

As I push her over and she gasps with delight, there's a naturalness between her movements that catches my attention—but not nearly so much as the naturalness to mine. It's the ease of being together with Baphomet that, more than any other piece of evidence, speaks to the truth in all her claims. Especially in the matter of her devotion to me, and the pleasure she takes in being near me. While she coos at the fingers I trail over her rear, I wonder how many times I've done all of this before with her. How many things I have done to her that humans simply could not do to one another? Whipping her with barbed wire while she strains in bonds of thorns—stuff like that. I bend to kiss her satin mouth, and as I do I strike against her rump with the belt.

"Master," she moans in shock, in pleasure, in anticipation. "Master! Yes, please, sir, oh—be strict with me. Make sure I never stray!"

"If I were me," I tell her, aiming a strike that snaps cruelly across the tops of her thighs and makes her kick her legs, "and I created you, then I would create you so you didn't have the capacity to stray."

"Oh! Mm—oh, sir, I would never dream of it—"

While I snap the belt a little higher, the leather licking sharply across labia peeking between her thighs and around the poor protection of the g-string, her tail whips through the air and her moans heighten sharply. I focus there, finding a rhythm she can enjoy, and while she pants beneath each snap of my belt I tell her, "Then why was the bartender able to tell you're a little slut?"

"Oh! Oh! Sir, everyone knows it…oh, everyone, man and woman, knows it to look at me…but—hm, hm, oh yes—when people see us together, oh, they'll know I'm *your* slut, Master! Only yours! Oh yes!"

I strike a bit harder all the time, and each time, my cock follows suit. Especially as, moaning desperately, she arches her rear in the air and begs, "Whip me, Master, please, oh, yes—beat me, choke me, use me—"

Damn…demon girls are something else. "Choke you, huh?"

She nods and whimpers on the bed. I pause only to strip off my clothes. As she wiggles eagerly out of her g-string, I tell her, "I can't kill you with this, can I?"

"No, sir, no, no! Oh, Master, we used to play these fun games all the time before you were sent to this place… mm, you used to strangle me until I passed out. I've missed it!"

Well, I might not go *that* far…not today, anyway. But seeing how eagerly she offers herself to me, pouting over her shoulder in that irresistible way, I feel inclined to give her at least a little of what she wants. Kneeling behind her, I swat along her ass with the belt a few more times before lassoing it around her throat—and lassoing is the right verb with those horns to consider. She gasps in excitement, reaching up to touch the leather strap as I slide against her soaking wet cunt.

"Yes! Mm, yes, please, Mas—ng!"

After looping the belt through its buckle at the nape of her neck, I yank it taut and ram my cock into her eager body. Her eyes roll up toward her forehead and I swear I see her pupils turn into hearts for at least a few seconds. As her tongue lolls out of her mouth, I groan a bit, myself. She tightens so sharply while the blood is cut off from her humanoid brain that I could practically explode right then. Instead, I loosen the belt and let her gasp for air for the next few seconds.

"Who's my good little sex slave?"

"Me, sir, me—awk!"

The belt tightens again and she trembles, her eyelids fluttering and her hands reflexively scratching at the leather strap. I've (consensually) choked some girls before, but, once again, it seems so natural and practiced with Baphomet. A few seconds later I loosen it, and she moans with absolute delight. Her tail, which tenses along with the belt each time I strangle her, relaxes and strokes over my chest. "That's right, Master, oh, that's right—oh, this brings back so many memories."

"I was just thinking something similar." While I yank again, her lolling tongue inspires me to renew the fervor of my fucking. With one hand holding the belt tight, I use the other to spank her. As she twitches around me in a sudden, sharp orgasm that's reflected in the wild kicking of her legs, I exhale and watch her. Her face is deep red but her swollen lips are smiling, and when I at last loosen the belt it seems to cause a second climax. As she flutters around me, I stroke her hair and then, feeling suddenly tender, caress her horns.

"Oh Master," she gasps, trembling, "oh, sir—"

"We must have fucked this way all the time…I feel like I've known you for years."

"You have! Oh—oh, Vic hasn't known me very long, Master, but *you've* known me my whole life…hm! Hm! Oh, sir!"

I fold my arms around her, forgetting the belt in favor of pressing her close to me and savoring every inch of her beautiful body. The heat of her well-whipped ass seems to make her especially fuckable, and as I stroke her horns and caress her breast I press my mouth to her ear.

"I wish I could share your memories," I tell her, my body tensing with the rising tide of the orgasm building in me. "I feel like everybody knows about me but me."

"Oh! Oh! Don't worry—oh, sir, we'll break all your

seals. You'll remember! You'll remember what a good, loyal slut I've always been…you'll remember that there's nothing for you to worry about—ah! Ah, ah! Master!"

Gritting my teeth, hastening my caresses of her horns, I pound home into her and that climactic tsunami. While it sweeps me away, I lower my head to nip her neck and inspire her matching orgasm. She screams with delight, squeezing around me even after she's taken every last drop I have to give her.

Once I've slid out, she collapses upon the pillow with a low moan and a noise like a purr.

"No wonder your rooms were close to mine," I tell her while drawing her limp form into my arms and stroking her hair between her horns. "You're the type of girl a man wants easy access to, Baphomet."

"You made me to be easy," she says with a pleased, crooked grin, a few strands of blonde hair sticking to the corner of her mouth. "I exist to serve you, Master…and I am happy that I do."

I'm sure that she is. But now, in the aftermath of lust, as I hold the contented demoness in my arms I can't help but wonder if her happiness means anything. If I created her to be my devoted slave, can she be said to have free will? If so, does that lessen her intrinsic value as a conscious being? Is she only some kind of flesh-bound automaton whose feelings are just a computer program's response to stimulus?

Maybe I'm only projecting. My mother does it all the time.

I am not looking forward to tomorrow.

FEBRUARY IS AN extremely temperate month in Tucson, though my mother still appears on her porch wearing a giant sun hat over her long auburn hair and a pair of enormous Audrey Hepburn sunglasses. I've decided to go without a jacket today. My tie remains, however, and I smooth it while making fun of her tendency toward over-protecting herself.

"Sunburns and skin cancer can happen all year-round," she chides me, making her way to the car. "Besides, how do you think I stay looking so hot?"

I snort and shake my head at that, but I do have to give it to her. For being a goofy nag in her fifties, she's still in pretty good shape and moves briskly to the passenger's seat. Her grin is heartwarming to me. It brings to mind a simpler place and time that's long-since passed me by.

"So," she says as I start the car and pull out on the road, "tell me all about work…"

The Gem and Mineral show is exactly as I remember it, and I have to admit that after a certain point my eyes glaze over. There are more gems and minerals out there than anybody needs to know about unless they're a mason or a new-age MILF…and, not fitting into either one of these categories, I can't help but find the show to be somewhat lacking in appeal over all. If you really want to keep your trade show alive, you have to find something to intrigue a broad array of consumers. Dinosaur teeth are about as cool as this place gets. At the very least, sensing my boredom, my mother tries to keep me entertained.

"So are you going to take this new sales job?"

I spread my hands. "I don't know, but I think so."

"Your father was very good in sales—a true professional. You could make real money in that kind of position, Vic! I think you've got what it takes."

"You've always thought I've got what it takes…even when I don't."

"Oh, stop, that's not true—look! Wow, oh, look at these cubes—"

She's off again, hurrying down a row of tables arranged with box on box of labeled rock. I laugh to myself, hanging back and sliding my hands into my pockets.

My fingers brush the sphere.

Why did I put it in my pocket when Beatrix came home? Frowning, I draw it from my trousers and study it in my hand—as much as something like this can be studied, anyway. Just like yesterday, my eye feels unable to settle upon it for longer than a second or two. Unable to find rest, my gaze naturally slides away every time until I am no longer staring at the stone but instead my fingers or the edge of my palm. It is a strange process that I am somehow not fully conscious of until I realize my focus is no longer where I put it.

Frowning, I turn it this way and that in the light. Despite what I can only describe as an ethereal gloss, still I find no reflection; no hint of true sun-beams shining on it. I have the sense I am holding a black hole—something I shouldn't look upon.

My mother calls out to me. Sniffing slightly, I slide the stone back into my pocket and go see what she wants to show me.

Being with my mother for the first time after the strange revelations of the week has an effect on me that I didn't expect. This world, my prison—it's my mother's world just as much as it's Despina's world. As much as it's anyone's. She doesn't just represent my physical connection to the planet as Vic Legion: she represents why this world is worth protecting. If it's true that, were I eliminated, this world would serve no purpose and be destroyed, the stakes are infinitely higher than I had considered before. By trying to kill me, the angels are trying to kill my mother.

And I may not be winning any son of the year awards any time soon, but I'm sure as shit not going to lie down and just let my mother's world disappear.

"Are you okay, sweetie?" She asks this around 4 PM, laying her hand on my arm and looking concernedly into my face. "You've been so *quiet* today. What happened this week?"

"I don't know," I say with a shake of my head. "It's really just too much to go into…but, I don't know."

Suddenly aware again of the stone in my pocket, I slide it out and extend it to her while she gasps. "Maybe I was just trying to decide the right time of the day to give you this."

"Oh, Victor! It's so beautiful, thank you! I didn't even see you buy it, you sneaky thing. Wow!" Taking it reverently out of my hand, Mom turns it over in her palm and marvels. "What kind of stone is it?"

"You know, I didn't ask."

"We should find the seller! Where did you buy it?"

"Ah, I can't remember by now." While my mother leans in for a kiss on my cheek, her reddish hair fluttering about her face in a gust of wind, I ask myself—is she really still my mother? Is she, isn't she? I vacillate between the two states constantly, always eventually choosing to embrace the concrete, static state where I say: Yes, she is my mother. Yes, I am still Victor Legion. Yes, I am more than my destiny.

And every time, a voice in the back of my head asks me, "Are you sure?"

Glancing briskly at my watch as she leans away to look at her treasure again, I tell her, "Besides—it's probably time to get going. My thing is at seven, and this is when the weirdos start to come out."

Scoffing, laughing, my mother slaps my arm with her free hand, but it's true. For whatever reason, the Tucson Gem and Mineral Show attracts about as many users of psychedelics and uppers as it does professional masons or private rockhounds. The last thing I want to do is be stuck here once the vibe starts to shift.

Besides…leaving is already a nightmare. The dirt lot being used for parking is crammed full of cars. I marvel at the scale of a show for rocks while trying to locate my Lincoln. Not too hard. The car is old, but well-kept and certainly better-washed than most of the cheap beaters filling the rows.

They make the Benz stick out like a sore thumb.

Gripping my mother's arm without even thinking, much as she once would throw her arm out across my chest when stopping short even well into my teenage years, I ignore her question—"What's wrong?"—and forcefully redirect her up the row we've nearly passed up.

"I think it's this way, actually," I tell her, but she (rightly) insists.

"No, honey, it was this way." With a gesture of her well-manicured hand and a jangle of colorful bangles around her wrist, Mom says, "You really need to pay more attention to where you park."

Scoffing, having to remind myself to not be actually insulted, I tell her, "Well I *did* pay attention, I know where I parked my car, and I can tell you that it's up this row."

My mother rolls her eyes and shakes her head—but, to my relief, lets me steer her up the aisle and out of sight of the Benz. "Well, one of us is about to feel pretty silly."

And I do feel pretty silly putting on a pantomime of failing to find the car, then admitting that she was right…but it's better than whatever the alternative is. My mother looks as smug as I would expect her to when I admit defeat on the opposite end of the long row, and from this safer vantage we pass the Benz and find my car where I left it.

Even with those precautions, did the driver see us? My head buzzes with conspiratorial concern. While I get the door for my mother to give me a few seconds of thinking, it occurs to me that driving her home could endanger her life. At the very least, it would give whomever was stalking me information that they didn't have before—and that they could use to their advantage.

In fact, maybe they already have that information. Maybe they followed me from my apartment in the morning and saw me pick my mother up. Had the person been in the show with us, following us on-foot, too? Had I just not seen?

Damn. I wish I could have Beatrix with me all the

time. Somebody watching my back is invaluable now.

While I start the car, my mother asks me, "Want to come hang out at home an hour before your party? I could throw together some dinner once I've had a few minutes to sit down!"

"Ah, you know, Mom, maybe, but—I was thinking we could go to dinner somewhere else, or something."

Creeping almost silently forward through the row, I keep as subtle an eye as I can in the Benz's direction. It hasn't started yet. I go a little faster and join traffic, my heart in my throat. By the time the vehicle in question is obscured, I haven't seen it make a move.

"Oh, that might be nice! I'm still a little full from lunch, though."

"Me, too."

What do I do, what do I do? What did I do the last time I saw this car? I fled and got lucky.

Well—not lucky, exactly. Really, I got my first glance of Despina.

"But, um"—I drive with one hand while shifting my phone from my pocket with the other, unlocking it and sorting through the contacts while my mother protests—"I know where we can, uh, can hang out and—"

"What are you *doing*, Victor! Pay attention to the road!"

"Sorry, just need to make a call."

While I lift the phone to my ear, neglecting to activate hands-free features just in case Despina says something untoward or doesn't immediately get the message, my mother grumbles unhappily. I ignore her. Despina picks up in two rings, which gives me a little thrill of power and a flare of desire to hear her voice.

"Is everything all right?"

"Hey babe," I tell her, feigning the casual and chipper

tone I've heard more functional men than I use on the women they're dating, "how are you tonight?"

The pause on the line tells me she's trying to figure out whether this is an error or some sort of compromised form of communication. Hoping she'll get that it's the latter, I go on, "That's great. Hey, uh, I was wondering—you said you wanted to meet Mom, right? That I should bring her over sometime? Well, there's an angel looking after us…we've got a couple of hours."

While my mother's ears perk, Despina gets the picture at least in part.

"Oh! Uh-huh, yep. Definitely, yes, bring her over right away."

"That's great! Can't wait to see you. Love you," I say in sing-song, trying to be as saccharine as possible to fit my mother's idea of what I'd ought to be like with a girlfriend. After hanging up with Despina, I pull off on the side of a road I deem safe and free of suspicious vehicles. With the hazards on, I quickly locate an e-mail confirmation from the taxi company's online order form and there find Despina's address. Upon punching this into my car's GPS, I pull back onto the road.

My mother, meanwhile, spends the whole time distracting me by demanding to know, "Since when did you have a girlfriend!"

"I'm always seeing girls, Ma."

"Oh, I know you're always *seeing* girls. But since when did you have a girl you saw more than once—let alone a girl you called your 'girlfriend?'"

I glance briskly at her. At what point do you tell your mother you have not one, but three girlfriends? And when does the demon part get added in? Yikes. Better do it before the holidays and give her some time to adjust.

"Despina's just a cool chick," I tell my mother, adding

genuinely, "I think you two will get along."

"You say that like I can't get along with anyone."

Yikes, not touching that one with a ten-foot pole. "Anyway, maybe we can just hang out with Despina for an hour or two. You can get to know each other, we can have dinner…"

The whole drive to Despina's safehouse, the Benz is nowhere to be seen. Once I've parked, my mother unfolds from the car with a stretch and an impressed look around the neighborhood. "What a nice area. What did you say she does for a living?"

"I didn't."

Without waiting for her to follow, I make my way over the graveled front yard to the door. I'm just about to knock when it opens to reveal Despina, looking a little breathless and very fucking hot in a pair of yoga pants, a hooded sweatshirt, and a grabbable ponytail. While my mind eagerly replays the sound of her calling me 'Master,' I smile.

"Hey, Despina." Loving that she has to play along even if she's all business inside, I slide my arms around her and draw her close to me. She does seem to barely stave off a tense expression…but her small smile and the hands she trails over my chest as I embrace her are plenty organic. I bend my head and press a kiss to her mouth, my tongue stealing briefly in before I lift my head to tell her softly, "Thank you."

"My pleasure," she responds *sotto voce,* turning away from me as I release her and step into the house. "And you must be—"

"Linda," my mother says, smiling to shake Despina's hand. "It's so wonderful to *meet* you! What a nice surprise this is."

"For me, too…there was just no warning at all."

"Tell me about it! Victor is always keeping me in the dark. What a lovely house you have!"

"Oh, thank you, I've really only just moved in…please, make yourself at home."

In a matter of minutes we're in the living room, where I take up post by the window. Occasionally I pace as far as the edge of the foyer before, arms crossed, I make my slow circuit back to my primary station.

What am I going to do about this? Is there *any* point at which it becomes safe for me to take my mother home? Do I have to figure out some way to convince her to stay the night here? She'll never agree to a hotel.

"So how did you two meet?" My mother looks between us, smiling all the while, until she sees me staring through the slats of the blinds. "Now, Victor, would you sit down and *relax?* You don't have to be so nervous. You look like you're at an inquisition."

"Sorry, I can't help it. To answer your question, Despina was doing security for Helcom and we just sort of hit it off. When her firm transferred her to another assignment, she said good-bye to me and I asked her out for a drink. Right, sweetheart?"

Despina looks relieved, not just by the fluency of my fiction but by my decision to refrain from developing it until I'm in front of her. Able to improv with me, she nods, her ponytail bouncing and yet not one single hair coming free of the bangs pinned in a preppy bump atop her head.

"Oh yeah." Despina bats her wing-tip lined eyes as she smiles at me in a fresh, sexy way that's a little wry but convincingly romantic. "Vic was my favorite person to see every morning. I just couldn't believe he would want to date me, though."

"Why not?" I stare intensely into her eyes from across

the room, savoring the blush that deepens the copper of her cheeks. "You're smart, beautiful, cool, athletic. I feel very lucky to have you."

With a shy little grin down at herself, Despina shakes her head and says to my mother, "See? He's a real charmer."

"Oh, he *is.*" Laughing, nursing the diet soda my friend has given her, my mother crosses her legs and smooths the black and white stripes of her skirt. "You should have seen him when he was a little kid. Adults would just bend over backward for him…of course, only I knew the truth. A real brat! He mostly grew out of it, though." With a wink and a grin over at Despina, she adds, "But you have to be sure to keep a man like him on a tight leash. Don't fall asleep at the wheel, now."

"Good God, Mother…"

Sighing, I glance out the window because it's an easier solution than finding some way to escape my body and the situation at-hand.

And as I look, the Benz comes crawling around the corner.

My eyes squeezing shut, I take advantage of a developing conversation between the women to slide my phone from my back pocket. Quickly, I send Despina a text.

> *Benz outside.*
> *I need to do something.*
> *Distract her for an hour or two for me.*

Then, even before Despina's phone buzzes in her sweatshirt with the response, I slide my phone away and announce, "You know, you guys are having such a great conversation—why don't I grab a bite to eat for us?"

My mother looks over, secretly pleased but acting reluctant to come off as more polite than she really is. "Oh, are you sure? Why don't we just order a pizza?"

"No, no, this is such a nice chat. How about I go get— you know what? Let me make it a surprise."

Hurrying over to my mother to kiss her cheek, then leaning down to embrace Despina while she glances at her phone and swipes something away, I tell them both, "I'll be back," and hope that's true.

"Hey," says Despina, hurrying after me into the foyer. "Wait, let me give you some money."

Much as I earlier steered my mother in the parking lot, Despina grips my arm with one firm hand. She drags me beyond the foyer, beyond the open kitchen, and into the secluded dining area that, lacking in cheerful decoration of any kind, is austere as a dollhouse freshly built.

"What are you going to do?"

I shake my head. "I don't know. But if there's even a remote possibility that my enemies know where my mother is living, I can't risk taking her home…and I would say there is a *substantial* possibility they know that information from following me today. If I want to get her out of here without her finding out what's going on, I or Baphomet or somebody else needs to face this angel down."

Lips pursing, Despina tells me, "Hold on," and disappears into an adjacent room. After a few noises like something being moved and something else being opened, she returns with a gun and two additional clips. "I'll breathe easier knowing you've got some form of protection while you're risking your life like this—but I don't think this is a good idea."

"I don't, either…but I don't have a better one. It's that, or convince her to hide out in my inter-dimensional apartment with my demon lover. But, well—if it comes to that, maybe you'll be down to come, too." While I wink at her, Despina manages an uneasy smirk. I smile slightly, affixing the gun's holster to my belt while she watches.

"Hey," she says as I thank her and turn away.

When I look back, Despina throws her arms around my neck and presses her mouth to mine. Exhaling, I embrace her tightly, almost crushing her fragrant body against mine.

When I hold her, I forget that I am not human inside.

"Be careful," she whispers, releasing me and slipping away to get the door.

"As careful as I can be," I respond, making my way out to my car and pausing before I get in.

No other moving vehicles in sight. I climb in and start the engine, waiting, listening. Nothing happens—no car comes careening right around the corner just to hear me get into my Lincoln—so I pull back out of the driveway and make my way back out of the development.

There's the car, waiting for me at the corner as I pull onto the street: watching the entrance of the development rather than the house itself. Every muscle in my body tense, I pass it by and get on the road to the highway. Suspicious that this proximity to an on-ramp is an intended feature of Despina's home, I wait until I catch my first glimpse of the Benz in my rear view. Only then do I call Beatrix's cell phone.

Baphomet picks up.

"Hello, Master. Are you on your way home?"

"I wish I were. That Benz that's been following me—I'm leading it to someplace where I have some room to fight."

Gasping, Baphomet says, "No, Master! By yourself?"

"I left my mother with Despina. I'm going to go

someplace where I can find a little space."

"The desert?"

"Too much space—you'd have a harder time finding us."

"Yes, yes, please wait for me if you can. Where are you going?"

I wasn't sure when I hit the road, but the farther I drive, the more it becomes evident that I'm heading back to the same highway I was on when I first encountered the stalker. While this settles in on me, I tell her, "The airplane graveyard on the south side of town, looks like. Meet me there as soon as you can."

"I'm on my way."

While she hangs up, I wonder if this gun is really going to be sufficient protection for me. Can a bullet kill an angel? I suppose that if a bullet can destroy a demon's human identity, it could destroy an angel's human identity as well. What would happen then? Would the angel or demon be forced to incarnate anew, or would it be completely destroyed, as seems to be thought the case with me—or, at least, with the world around me?

I can only hope there will be no way back for an angel once its corporeal form has been exterminated.

When I'm finally down by the airplane graveyard, my pursuer is about five cars behind me on the road. I've seen him change lanes at least once, probably straining for a better glimpse of me. I hope he sees it as I pull sharply off the road and to the shut gate of a property whose breaking and entering is surely about seven or eight different federal offenses.

But I just can't be made to care right now. The car barrels right through the padlocked gate and I don't even think about it. My intuition tells me that being arrested should not be even close to the top of my list of concerns—

that, for me, it's not a risk. I've always felt that way, that sense of pre-ordained permission to do as I wished with few or no consequences, but now that feeling is justified in a way it's never been. It's a fine line between hubris and confidence, but if you don't have faith in yourself, you can't take the risks required to excel in life.

Sometimes, even to survive.

While I slam the brakes and the car screeches to a halt, I clamber out of the Lincoln and draw the gun. Just as the Benz pulls up twenty yards behind me, I get the safety off.

I don't wait.

While the door opens, I fire a round at the driver's side of the windshield, then yank open the rear driver's side door of my vehicle to gain a bit of cover. While I fire off a wild shot and then crouch out of sight, I'm finally justified in my week of paranoia. Another crack of gunfire answers mine, and I know I've been right to take all this seriously.

The window above me cracks and, on the second bullet, shatters.

What's worse, both impacts occur with little bursts of bright green light whose boundaries are marked by some sort of sigil.

It reminds me of the mark behind Despina's ear, but only in the most unconscious of ways. As one may imagine, I'm a little distracted…and regretting my decision to go without a jacket. I throw my arm over my head and curse not my own welfare but the car's, incredibly annoyed to have to even think about taking this thing back to the garage, and lean around my cover to discharge a few bullets of my own. Though the Benz's door stands up to the conventional gunfire, I'm pleased— and, I admit, somewhat surprised—to see how true my aim is. In a brief experiment, I try to hit the side view window and succeed in knocking it off the door.

I've been shooting once or twice before, but certainly not under conditions like these. Is this more general evidence of my true nature—or is it, like my sudden talent for fist-fighting the other day, the sign of another seal?

Whatever it is, I'm not going to complain.

When the gun clicks empty, I duck back down and switch the old clip out for a new one. As I chamber a bullet, however, a footfall draws my attention. I look up in time to see a suited man appear around the back of my car, where he must have crept to during my brief blitz of gunfire. He's a Black man, a guy about the size and broad shape of the one who clocked me from behind when I was dealing with the angel in the alley.

I don't believe in coincidences anymore.

Quickly, I lift my pistol and fire. His gun flies out of his hand. He swears, watches it skid away, then—to my horror—keep coming at me. I manage to squeeze off one un-aimed shot in his general direction, but his movements are too fast. He grabs hold of my gun and, while struggling to wrench it from my hand, bares his teeth with the exertion. I try not to look too amazed that he has to fight me this much.

"Don't fight this, Legion," he says while we wrestle for the weapon. "It's better this way."

"It's one thing when you angels are stalking me in the street and following me all around town—it's another thing when you threaten my mother."

"Your mother will be put out of her misery if you're killed," says my opponent, drawing back his head and cracking mine so sharply my eyes water. "It's the kindest thing for her! For anyone."

At last he manages to get the gun from my hand; and I scramble into my car and shut the door on his wrist. While he howls with pain, I squeeze into the front seat and shift it from park to drive. The Lincoln surges forward.

My assailant just barely manages to extricate his hand before he's dragged along.

I floor it, peeling off down the road, and grimacing for my tires while the car does an about-face.

As he fires I swerve, wince through the spider-webbing of my windshield, and ram the car into him dead-on.

While the crunch of metal and bone fills the air, the man's eyes burn with red fire.

I REALIZE ONLY after a few long seconds that the entity stalking me has been a demon. Everyone spent so much time assuming it was an angel that the signal of his red eyes doesn't click until he pushes himself up from the crumpled hood with a groan. A ribbon of blood splatters from his mouth to the metal.

While he raises the gun, I shift the car to reverse.

He catches hold of the bumper and the tires whine uselessly, his burning eyes finding mine through the cracks of my windshield.

Something careens from the sky, a meteor of wild flames I realize is Baphomet only when I get a glimpse of horn. Jerking his head up toward the motion, my opponent raises his gun, but—too late. Gripping him by the shirt, flinging him away from the car, Baphomet bares her fangs and spreads her arms to collect fire from her wings.

"Asmodeus," she snarls with disdain, throwing great fistfuls of fire at the demon disguised as a man. "I should have known it would be you! I would have thought eternity would be long enough to cool your jets, but I'm not surprised…you've always been a weak-willed traitor."

"Why should we all be punished for what he did," says the demon, raising his human arm amid waves of purple energy that form a powerful shield. While Baphomet's flames roll off around all sides of the barrier, he stares through the chaos and into me. "We were fooled. There's no reason for us to all be compelled here along with him."

"You made your choice when you joined our ranks! No matter what you do to please the angels, they'll never accept you as one of their own again."

While Asmodeus fires off one of the few rounds remaining in my pistol, I glance around. His gun, lost in the middle of the road, waits to be useful. While my demonic concubine rockets up into the sky, her flaming wings beating a whirlwind that whips our opponent off his feet, I sprint to the gun and snatch it up.

And I *feel* it in my brain.

The gun is not a normal gun. I knew that by its bullets, but now to hold it I'm close enough to distinguish its queer characteristics. Letters in a language I don't know are written down the barrel, and the muzzle is ringed in a sigil I will find to be like the one on the bullets when I have the leisure to practice shooting.

Most notably to me at the time, the chamber, once glowing the same acid green as the previous bullets, shifts to a rich indigo blacklight while I feel a kind of tap into the front of my mind. I can find no other way to describe it than by comparing it to how a tree must feel when humans tap it for sap.

Like fingers, roots of some kind, have wiggled into the

tingling front of my brain and opened a new channel for the expenditure of energy.

Experimenting, I raise the gun and fire it at the Benz's hood three times. The immaculate vehicle's front end crumples, untold damage done to the exterior and interior of the idling innocent until, at the third shot, it bursts into flames.

Asmodeus glances over sharply, his teeth bared to reveal fangs not unlike Baphomet's—and then he sees me, still holding the smoking gun.

He raises my pistol without a word, but Baphomet hurls a fireball that roars over and around him like the mouth of a terrible lion. Snarling, Asmodeus lifts his arms too late and takes a terrible sear across the right side of his face. Flesh blisters so severely that I can even tell from a distance. He cries out, fumbling the weapon: but, while he drops the gun, he experiences a change more severe than third degree burns.

Asmodeus's demonic transformation is altogether more horrible than the charming, somehow kitschy one that Baphomet uses to become Beatrix, or vice versa. Wings of an energy as evil and thick as an oil slick shoot out from his back, and the frill that extends back from his head reminds me of a lizard—or a dragon.

"I'll be back for my gun," he hisses, spiraling into the air and then, with a sonic crack, jetting off faster than my human eye can follow.

My heart beating so fast I'm dizzy, I stand in the middle of the airplane graveyard with this magical gun in my hand. I feel like I don't even know what's just happened.

Panting, her defensive posture relaxing somewhat to see him fly off, Baphomet makes sure that he's gone and spends a few seconds collecting herself.

Then, to my shock, she whirls on me with tears in her eyes.

"You *idiot!*"

My eyes widen along with my mouth. At once she's upon me, her dainty fists pounding on my chest, a sob in her voice.

"I told you," she says, "I *told* you to be careful, you big, stupid idiot! Why would you do this by yourself?"

"Baphomet—"

"No! No excuses! You should have called me the second you realized something was wrong. You should *always* call me, Master!"

Clutching the front of my shirt, tears streaming down her exhilarated face, Baphomet gazes up at me and says, "If something happened to you, and I wasn't around to help—I don't know what I'd do. Ah!"

The mere thought makes her weep with absolute heartbreak.

I'm shocked.

While she nuzzles her face against my chest as much as her horns will allow, I slide the magical gun into Despina's holster and fully embrace Baphomet.

"Please," she says with a little sob. "I love you, Master. I never want to lose you again."

I see.

My thoughts from the night before come rushing back to me, a kind of unexpected shame poisoning the molecules of my body to remember how cruelly I had suddenly felt toward her. I had let the idea that I created her blind me to the richness of her existence—a kind of hollow solipsism that embarrasses me as I realize it. The reality is that, created by me or not, created to be in love with me or not, Baphomet is an independent being with a rich internal emotional life.

Perhaps one richer than mine.

Arms tightening around her, I lower my head and squeeze my eyes shut.

"I'm sorry, Baphomet," I tell her, feeling a little misty to be faced with the purity of her love. "I never should have doubted you. Let's rely on each other a little more from now on, okay?"

Nodding, Baphomet leans away from me and wipes her cheeks. "I just want you to be safe."

Patting her head between the horns, I bend, kiss her brow, then tell her, "We should go."

"*You* should go," she corrects me, looking up into the sky, then at my ruined car. Frowning, she reaches out and touches it. A similar red light to the one that healed my hands expands across its surface. As the metal smooths and the glass appears to grow back, she says in a now faintly woozy voice, "I have to get to the pool tournament. But be careful, Master. Promise?"

"I promise. It'll all be fine now, Baphomet—don't worry."

Her brow furrowed even at my reassurance, she forces herself to nod. With a similar rocketlike take-off into the air, Baphomet rises up into the sky and jets off to the north.

Alone, I recover Despina's gun and am down the highway quite a ways before I even see emergency responders rushing to the scene. Infernal providence, or interference? I can't think it's only luck.

Though, I have to admit…I am feeling lucky. Now having seen Baphomet in action, I realize what a powerhouse she is—and how invaluable she is in more senses than a sexual one. I wonder what she can tell me about this gun?

After examining it in Despina's holster at a stoplight,

I slide it under my seat and place her normal weapon into it.

How exhausting! Must be the adrenaline…I feel so drained I don't even know if I can make it to nine, let alone to the end of a department pool tournament made to facilitate long hours and lots of drinking. Leaning back in my seat, I pull up Despina's address on the GPS, then let it and highway hypnosis do the rest while my brain tries to sort out everything that's happened. These sessions of introspection are becoming a regular requirement.

Maybe I need a good therapist…if one exists to deal with situations like this.

I guess I could always manifest one, huh?

Is manifesting a person as easy as manifesting an object?

What about a magical object? This magical gun, say? Could I manifest that as easily as I manifested my mother's rock?

At Despina's house, I hit the doorbell and wait. She throws it open, her tension releasing to see me. While she throws her arms around my neck and I embrace her in return, my mother calls from the living room, "There he is! What'd you bring for dinner, Vic?"

Ah, fuck.

THE NEXT HOUR is a blur. I spend it dashing to a nearby burrito place, returning to my baffled and disappointed mother (and far more sympathetic friend), then fidgeting restlessly while I wait for Mom to decide she's ready to go.

Unfortunately, she and Despina have been getting along exceedingly well. I practically have to drag her from the house while she continues trying to hug and kiss the first girlfriend of mine she's met since I was in high school.

"Let's go shopping sometime," she calls while I cram her into my car, waving and blowing more kisses. Laughing, Despina waves after her and casts me one final look of intrigue. Indicating nothing, she disappears back into her house. My mother does not notice the glance, as she is too busy smiling to herself while hunting through her purse for her phone.

"Oh, what a *sweetheart* she is. You've got a good one there…and a real cutie!" Opening her phone to send a text message to Despina, (and she wonders why I don't introduce her to my girlfriends), she fits her sunglasses atop her mane of red hair and says, "Why, if I were your age…"

"Mom!"

My mother cackles while I pull sourly out of the development. "*Well?* She's a hottie. Consider yourself lucky you're my son instead of my daughter…I'd probably end up stealing all your boyfriends."

"Just what went on while I was out?"

"I don't know, Vic."

We pull up to a red light and my mother's sharp eyes, piercing hazel daggers, flip toward me. My palms dot with sweat. I remember being ten and I swear she even seems a little bigger in the seat beside me.

"What did go on while you were out?"

I scoff, glancing out the window before looking ahead at traffic.

"So," I say after a second, "what'd you think of the burrito?"

Her playful facade slips back into place and she beams at the thought of it. "My, my! It was awfully delicious… maybe could have been a bit spicier, though…"

The conversation goes on. I feel like I've dodged the first bullet, but that there are more on the horizon. Sooner or later, I'm going to have to tell her the truth about some of this.

Especially if I'm going to keep her safe.

As we approach her house, Despina remains the subject of discussion. "Can you *believe*," says my mother, appalled, "that she's never been to the Gem and Mineral sho—oh, no!"

With a sad gasp, Mom sorts through her purse and then shuts it, despondent. "Oh, shit! I forgot your stone at her house! Oh, honey, I'm sorry."

"You just want an excuse to drop in on her sometime."

"I really did forget it! We were just having such a fun conversation…and then you got all impatient and dragged me out. You won't be *that* late to your little to-do, will you?"

I glance at the clock, trying to suppress my annoyance. 7:40…I should have dropped off dinner and given Despina the gas money to drive her home.

After promising my mother I'll get her stone back to her eventually, I hustle over to Frank's Bar and have to park two blocks down. The magical gun still sits under the driver's seat. I triple-check that my doors are locked before making my way back to the site of the company pool tournament.

Then, with a glance down at myself to make sure I'm not too covered in debris to be presentable, I enter the bar and am quickly greeted by a bevy of happy voices.

"Vic!" Mike calls to me from across the packed establishment. He's not at our usual seats on the left side but instead off to the right, where the pool tables are rendered almost invisible by the sea of Helcom employees. I smile and wave at a few people before diving into the crowd and eventually coming up for air near my work friend.

"I wasn't sure you were going to make it," he says, bumping fists with me.

"Too bad I missed the sign-ups for the tournament," I respond dryly, wiping a non-existent tear from my eye.

Mike's grin is eviler than any expression made by the demon I fought earlier today. "Not to worry," he crows to my immediate displeasure. "I wasn't sure if you'd be here in time for sign-ups, so I took the liberty of putting your name down…your game will be up next, the last in the round."

"Oh great," I say through playfully clenched teeth. "Great, thank you, what a pal you are."

"Aren't you glad we're friends?" With a jovial laugh and a sip of his beer, Mike then uses his glass to gesture and say, "Anyway, you're just in time. Look who's playing!"

His gesture points to none other than Beatrix. Her waves of sunshiny hair are pulled back behind her neck and her suit jacket is MIA. While she bends over, every eye in the room is drawn to the luscious shape of her hindquarters beneath the embrace of her high skirt. Her perfectly honed legs are among the longest and most statuesque I have seen, and her face rivals any Renaissance portrait committed to canvas by Da Vinci.

And she is not just mine: she is my creation, a walking song of my heart, a lover as much as a daughter as much as a protector. Minerva, straight out of Jove's head. She is a radiant envisioning who makes me burn with gratitude and confidence, and when she looks up from sinking the 8 with a cheer, she locks eyes with me and showers me in a smile that brings a surge of warm affection through my breast.

"Well done," calls Mike, applauding next to me. I applaud along with him, smiling at the disguised demoness who grins amid her curtsey. When the applause break, long-absent Gabe appears from the crowd with a few claps of his own.

"Very good game! All right, people…let's have our final round one match-up. Round two can start over there—Vic? Did Vic make it?"

Helpfully pointing, Mike calls, "He's over here!"

Looking around for me, then smiling in a way that

seems somehow sardonic, Gabe says, "Oh, good! I see you made it after all. Well, this should be interesting! Care to take a guess at who you'll be playing?"

I let him see at least a hint of the annoyance surging in me.

"You, right?"

Gabe's grin widens.

"Pick a cue," he says, gesturing to the wall. "Any cue."

With a withering glance at traitorous Mike, I make my way over to the wall and decide between the pool cues. Though I'm pretty decent at pool, I'm not exactly a tournament champion and have to roll a few on the table before I find one that doesn't seem bent.

Then, while working some chalk on the end of my chosen cue, I scoff. Gabe has produced a carrying case and removed a custom stick from within. As he screws it together I exchange a look with Mike and Beatrix, both of whom either roll their eyes or shake their heads.

"Some kind of pool hustler, are you?" I ask this wryly of Gabe.

"I dabble," my manager responds to the laughter of the crowd.

And I laugh, too…but, thanks to the affectation of mirth that draws my attention to his crinkling eyes, I notice something odd. Discoloration from being sick, maybe? He looks somehow drained, but I can't put my finger on it. The coloring around his eyes just seems off somehow. Matte. He doesn't sound sick, though, and doesn't move like a sick man, either.

In fact, he's a shark from the break. When he sends the balls rollicking around and right away sends the four into a side pocket, I know I'm in for the fight of my life.

"So was this pool tournament your idea?"

"Oh no," he says, lining up his next shot and bending

over to expertly snap the two into a corner pocket, a shot that he calls before saying, "but I thought it sounded like fun!"

Yeah, I'll bet he did. His third shot just barely avoids going in, springing off the pocket's edge and whirling back toward its center like a planet through space. Studying the remaining odd balls, I take my best shot and sink a three. Mike and Beatrix clap for me, but the thrill is short-lived. With too much enthusiasm behind my arm, I send the cue ball into the pocket.

My stomach sinks.

Gabe and I make sharp eye contact. My opponent senses my weakness and snatches the white ball from the corner pocket.

The ridges of my knuckles whiten while my fists tighten around the cue.

"Now don't let yourself get distracted, Legion." After deciding best how to arrange his ball, he sets it down and takes his shot without thinking about it for more than a second or two. "You don't want to make this too easy for me, do you?"

The ball goes in, but the next doesn't, and he leaves an easy side pocket for me. By this point most of the shindig is following our game, ignoring the round two players entirely and gradually shifting attention to us. And I understand why—we're good, very good, and a good game of pool is great to watch—but I wish they'd look elsewhere, because I become acutely aware of the pressure to beat the manager. Especially when I get a good chain and sink three balls in one turn. His falling face is a thing of beauty. The way he smiles when I finally miss is too annoying to stand.

Eventually, by the grace of the pattern into which we fell and a missed shot that Gabe looks a little pissed about, I end up sinking my last ball before Gabe gets a shot at his.

I inhale, exhale. Beatrix and Mike are on the edges of their seats, understanding that now is not the time to cheer. When I align my shot, it seems like the whole room has stopped breathing.

Gabe watches me closely. Sweat dots his forehead from the tension of the game.

I strike.

The 8-ball rockets toward its destination, looking to be on perfect target.

In an eyeblink before it hits the pocket, it diverts course and bounces off the edge of the table.

My jaw drops. Beatrix sits up in her seat and looks at me sharply, her expression not dissimilar to mine. When I whip around to look at Gabe, he purses his lips and furrows his brow in a poor imitation of sympathy.

"Oo," he says while the room around groans with mortal agony, "too bad! Must be a bump in the felt there."

Sucking a tooth, saying nothing, I step back from the table.

At last, Gabe gets his shot at the 8.

My palms sweat. He drops his last even ball, then lines things up with leisure. The room is quiet.

He pops the cue into the black ball.

Down it goes.

The room, which I now realize has been rooting for me, moans in disappointed unison and resumes their conversations or returns their attention to the other game.

"Well," Gabe says, looking pleased with himself, his hands folded around the cue as he regards the empty table, "that was much closer than I expected it to be. Good game, Legion!"

With a gregarious smile, he extends his hand. "Better luck next time…if you won't have left us for sales by then," he adds with a wink. Is that what I look like when I wink? I better knock it the fuck off. "Don't sneak out of Mass after Communion, though—there's still plenty of fun to be had."

My mind simply overflows with the many delights afforded one by a company party. Biting my tongue, forcing a smile, I look down at my sweaty hand. What the fuck is that on there? Is he wearing paint of some kind?

"Break a leg in your next round," I tell him while I duck away without putting back the cue. He can do it if the next guy doesn't want it. It's his reward. That's what my mother always used to say when I won a board game: "First prize is cleaning up."

I admit I've always been a sore loser…but at least I come by it honestly.

Beatrix, though, looks even sorer, and fumes as I return to her and Mike.

"He was cheating," she says stonily while I slide between them, Mike noticing this with a look of withering envy and slight annoyance. I don't hold it against him. He'll understand eventually.

How much he'll understand, though, I don't know. Certainly nothing about my true nature, or hers. With a wave of his hand toward the table, he says, "There's no possible way Gabe could have bumped the table from where he was standing! He was like a foot away. He's right, the felt on these tables is just bad."

"They're old," I say.

Beatrix looks at me significantly, then leans across me with a warm smile for Mike. "Whatever. Mike"—she touches his arm in a casual but friendly way—"if I give you a few bucks, will you buy a round for the three of us?"

Flushed around the cheeks, barely glancing at his still half-full beer, Mike springs from his seat. "Oh, uh, don't worry about it! It's my treat. The least I owe Victor for forcing him to live through that."

"Maybe if you had bought me the beer a little sooner it would have helped."

Remembering the stuff on my hand, I look around for a napkin and find one on the bar. I distractedly blot the flesh-colored paint away while Beatrix leans toward my ear. Her voice is a whisper that raises goosebumps of desire down my neck on most other occasions, but which here fires my blood in a different way.

"Gabe is an angel," she tells me.

I LOOK SHARPLY at Beatrix upon hearing her absurd claim, still mechanically wiping my hand. She shakes her head to indicate I shouldn't react more than I already have. It is difficult to keep from peering over at Gabe, however.

Is this an angel, really? This jocular, goofy, slightly overweight simp?

Well…I guess before the start of this week I wouldn't have taken myself for a demon lord, either.

When he's moving about the table with his next competitor, I use advantageous angles to take a closer look at him. No—there's no way of discerning that he's anything but human.

"Are you sure?"

At my whisper, she nods. My lips tighten. How long have I worked for Gabe and the company? I just don't understand. I have these memories, these vague impressions of events, but I have no timeline upon which to affix them. Is it just some form of amnesia triggered by traumatic events, or by the awakening of my human self to my true nature? Is it a curse of some kind? Or is it really the case that this world only came into existence to maintain me in an unconscious state, hoping to keep my human vessel from awakening until it was too late for me to achieve my destiny?

It feels like there's some kind of conspiracy at work now. My own thoughts seem to me to be a form of schizophrenia. Here I am proposing that capitalism, and 9-to-5 workdays five days a week with little to no sick time and barely sufficient vacation, and commercials on cable TV, and propaganda infused into corporatized fiction, and stigmatized psychedelics, and wars, and social exploitation of all kinds, all exist to prevent the development of a supreme demon lord's consciousness—and that said demon lord just happens to be me.

But I guess it's not me that's proposing it. I guess it's my girlfriend, my loyal and lovely demoness companion who lets her knee brush mine while she leans forward to take her drink from Mike. She thanks him, and I thank him, and we drink and stew. We talk to Mike—or Beatrix does, anyway, entertaining like a geisha, taking up the burden of conversation for me so I can think.

She is truly the perfect concubine, and with no one looking or caring I slide my hand into the small of her back. Mike sees but does not comment. He seems to assume I am sore over my loss because he mostly talks to Beatrix and lets me brood in silence.

Who else in my life has been an angel all this time? I go through a list of names, struggling to remember everyone from teachers to long-forgotten pediatricians. It makes me feel truly insane. Yes, I am insane. This is true from a legal standpoint and certainly a social one. If I proposed any of these thoughts to any humie in the room, I'd end up in a straitjacket.

It is a relief to have Beatrix. Despina, too. Thinking of Despina makes me think of the gun still in my car, and then I wonder if I should avoid thinking about the gun right now. What are the limits of celestial powers? Can angels perceive thought? Are their powers limited by their human forms?

The image of the ball suddenly darting into the edge of the table, as if nudged by an invisible finger, flies back across my mind's eye.

"I'm gonna go smoke," I say, leaving my glass behind and heading out of the bar.

I can tell Mike wants to follow me, but Beatrix keeps him talking. Outside, I light a cigarette.

Is Gabe a present threat to my existence? Furthermore, if he is an angel, what does that say about the rest of Helcom's management team? Is Raphael in sales also an angel?

With that name, maybe. Are the other workers? Is that why Beatrix says there's such an inundation of celestial energy that she couldn't get a bead on it until we were in smaller numbers?

I'm just thinking about whether I should risk getting the gun when the back door of the bar opens.

Laughing along with another manager, Gabe steps into the smokers' area, then sees me with a briefly changed expression. His phone in his hand as though he were only coming out to make or take a call, he pauses, smiles, and says, "Legion! Having a good night?"

"Sure," I say, tossing my cigarette upon the asphalt and grinding it beneath the leather of my shoe. "It's been a real blast."

Though I try to pass him by without further comment, he stops me by touching my shoulder.

A sensation like a powerful static shock pops between our bodies.

Amid the crackle that I can feel all the way up to my scalp, a vast sigil bursts like fireworks between us: an iron-toned light that boldly gleams, then fades out fast as a sparkler. I don't have to ask what it is or whether or not the humie over there saw it. He clearly didn't, but I know I'm not imagining things. I saw it with my own two eyes—felt it, too—and even recognized the astronomical symbol in its center.

That was the Seal of Mars, the second of the seven planetary seals keeping me disempowered on this Earth—and the archangel Gabriel seems to be its keeper.

"I hope you're not sore about losing in there."

"I'd probably take it better if you hadn't been cheating," I tell him, staring hard into his beady eyes. While the other manager makes a displeased noise, Gabe scoffs lightly.

"I beg your pardon?"

"You heard me. I saw that ball. The felt on the tables is bad, but not enough to do something like that. We sank plenty of balls in that corner pocket. None of them did that until it counted. It seems to me like something interfered."

"But what? You saw me. I stood well clear from the table. How could I have possibly done something to redirect the course of the ball?"

"You know, Gabriel"—I cast one last glance toward the other manager—"I really couldn't say."

With a light sniff and a displeased look to be accused of such a thing in front of a third party, Gabe smiles thinly. "Well! Maybe we could play a rematch. Outside of the tournament, you know, once everybody else goes home. Just to soothe your ego."

Beatrix's words come wafting back to me: that a seal can be broken not just by physically defeating a seal-holder, but by overcoming a challenge.

"All right," I tell him, nodding in agreement. "I think I can stick around."

Forcing himself to maintain a smile, Gabe nods. "Hopefully that will settle your mind."

Now feeling a kind of anticipation rather than any brand of paranoia or dread, I make my way back into the bar. Just within the hallway, I pause and remove my phone. Despina's contact is still open when I go to my text messages.

> *Can't confirm,*
> *but you should watch*
> *area around Frank's Bar.*

> *Bring Mom's stone, too, please.*

When somebody comes around the corner to go to one of the bathrooms, I stuff the phone away and return to Beatrix and Mike.

"Looks like I'll be here awhile after all," I say to them both. "We're having a rematch."

"Ah, man!" Sighing in disappointment, Mike finishes his beer. "I'd love to stick around and watch, but I have to jet. I'm exhausted!"

"That's too bad." Frowning, Beatrix leans forward and hugs him in a brief way, then settles back into her seat beside me. "We'll tell you all about how it goes on Monday, I'm sure!"

"I'm sure you both will," says Mike with a more

meaningful glance toward me, promises of future conversations communicated in his arched brow. With a pat of my shoulder, he gets himself gone, and soon Beatrix and I settle in to watch the pool tournament.

Neither one of us cares about being seen together, suddenly. Not like it matters. I, for one, have decided I am going to take Raphael up on his offer to change departments. Even if he is an angel like Gabriel, he hasn't been actively pulling the wool over my eyes for an indeterminate amount of time.

Though it does make me wonder if I will ever be able to leave Helcom and still retain peace of mind. If there's really a whole organization of angels here, I can't justify just ignoring it and putting my life at stake.

Much better to climb to the top and purge the ranks accordingly.

"He's keeping a seal," I murmur in Beatrix's ear when we have a few safe seconds to exchange conversation. Her face tenses to hear such a thing. "I think it was Mars. Do they appear in a linear order?"

"Not necessarily."

"What does it signify?"

"Battle."

Oh, well now. That could come in handy. I go on to ask her, "Why did I see it just now when he touched me outside? He shook my hand after the pool tournament and I didn't notice anything."

"Because you've learned he is an angel since then," she answers. "I told you…the closer you get to the seal and its owner, the more obvious it becomes. It is about consciousness and knowledge. Focused attention."

Gabe returns and, though her whispering stops, Beatrix turns to me with a flirtatious smile. Her voice raises to a normal level. "I know you just went outside, but could I bum a smoke?"

"I'll come with you," I tell her.

We're just around the corner and out of sight when she draws me into the back office, then shuts the door behind me. "I just had to fuck you right now," she begs, pawing at the front of my trousers.

"Why now?"

"Oh, Master, because we need to increase our energy if we're going to win a fight with an angel tonight."

Her free hand frames my face as she lunges up for a kiss, quickly freeing me from my trousers before lifting high her leg. As usual, too horny to delay even to take her thong off, Beatrix pushes the little string aside and rubs her wet cunt against my length. I groan, pressing her back against a nearby desk. Her legs spread and her eyelids flutter with the anticipation of pleasure.

"Yes, Master, oh, yes, please—if you have to use that gun, you need this as much as I do. It takes more energy with each shot, you have to be sure you're ready to go."

"What an unbelievable slut you are…are you this wet from showing off this sexy body all night?"

"No, Master…oh, sir, I'm wet from being near you…I love men seeing me with you." She grins, a lock of blond hair falling across her cheek as I tease her with pressure from my cock. "Mm, oh, they all want me…but only you can ever have me. Ah—!"

She nearly screams as I slam myself deep into her pussy, but I'm quick to slap my hand over her mouth and muffle all her cries. While her eyes roll in their sockets, I bang her as quietly as I can upon the rattling desk while still satisfying our need for rough, passionate fucking. Even when I'm grateful to her for saving my life, my instinct is still to be brutal with Beatrix…maybe because I know that's how she wants it.

"You're a dirty little cocktease, slave," I grunt in her ear, each eager clench around my cock another throb of pleasure in my mind and another two IQ points temporarily lost. "All the guys at the office are going to be jealous of me…the women, too."

"Yeah—yeah—oh, let them be jealous, sir—oh, Master, oh Master, oh, Daddy, Daddy!"

It never ceases to amaze me how suddenly and sharply Beatrix cums. She really is ready to be fucked all day every day. It's irresistible…a demoness in heat is a hard partner to turn down. While she pants her way through her orgasm, her pussy rapidly convulsing around me, I tug her head back by the hair and kiss her mouth with fierce affection.

"Get on your knees, slut. Let's make this quick."

"Yes! Yes, sir, thank you, sir…" Beaming, nodding, Beatrix dismounts and scrambles down upon her feet. With a devious glance up at me, she runs her tongue along my shaft from base to head. "Mm, oh, Master… what a beautiful cock you have…"

Soon she's got it in her mouth again, pressing back and back into the depths of her unending throat. I groan, one hand patting and stroking her golden head while she bobs rapidly over me. My breathing shallow, my consciousness focused entirely in my sense of touch, I savor Beatrix and her sluttiness, her exhibitionism. To see her coveted by other men is how a king must feel when the rings upon his hand draw admiration from serfs who see in their miserable lifetime only those pieces of gold, and only during special holiday processions. Beatrix is a sublime experience to be known by none but me—and, of course, by the ladies I feel like sharing her with.

This is why I have to get rid of these fucking angels. Who needs some big apocalyptic war? Despina is right.

If I'm a demon lord, I want to enjoy my status. I want to surround myself with gorgeous women, I want to eat fine food and see all the corners of the world.

I want to live forever, no matter what it takes.

The footfall outside of someone passing the office on the way out to smoke tenses my body in a brief surge of anxiety, and at the next expert flicker of Beatrix's tongue, I spill down her throat and produce a low, rolling groan from the both of us.

"Good girl," I murmur, stroking her hair as she suckles the tip of my cock and squeezes every last drop into her mouth. "What a good little fuck-slave you are…that's right, ah, no wonder you're my favorite, baby…"

Giggling, she wipes the corner of her mouth and rises to her feet. After sliding her panties back on, Beatrix says, "Wait thirty seconds," and exits to the bar.

Dizzy, I tuck myself back into my trousers, wait another twenty-five seconds, and follow her.

I encounter no one. Like the airport graveyard, there are no consequences for my actions…except for a sidelong glance from Frank as I come around the corner, which I ignore like a guilty kid who skips school and later that day walks past his teacher's house.

Back in the thinning department tournament, Beatrix perches on her stool. She fixes her lipstick, touching up a smudged crimson edge in her compact.

As I sit back down, I pick up my beer. My nose wrinkles when I realize some of Gabe's flesh-colored paint managed to avoid my napkin and was instead transferred to the glass.

I almost comment on it to Beatrix, and in fact am looking over at her to do so, when she screws the cap back on her lipstick and drops it into her purse.

My mouth opens.

Peering across the bar at Gabe, I squint to see his hands mid-play, then check them against the strange matte tone around his eyes. I pat Beatrix's arm, show her the smear on the glass, then nod in Gabe's direction.

"Concealer," I whisper in her ear.

13

BEATRIX'S FACE SCREWS into a look of confusion, but I'm not confused at all. Everything clicks into place and I look back at Gabriel.

Now that I see it, he's definitely wearing concealer— and its grayish caste is the telltale sign of a poorly disguised shiner, like the one I gave to the angel stalking me before Despina saved my ass for the second time.

My own boss is my assailant: there's no doubt. Even his hands bear a few scrapes and bruises, which have peered through the smearing concealer as a consequence of wiping sweat from his brow and shaking hands with his competitors. Add to that his mysterious string of absences in the days before the tournament he's been harping on for a month, and suddenly I am more ready to kick his ass than ever.

The tournament drags on. Gabe loses his next match, thrown off by our confrontation outside of the bar. Incredibly, it's 10:30 by the time the final game is over. Those remaining are either bootlickers hoping for a promotion or people who are just too drunk to worry about getting home until they absolutely have to.

"Sure you don't want to save this for another day?" Gabe looks pointedly at his watch as I push myself away from the bar, where I've been lurking and occasionally murmuring to Beatrix. He glances over at her, either seeing if she intends to leave or lumping her in with me—perhaps as able to sense her demonic nature here as she is able to sense is celestial one.

"I don't feel like dragging this out," I tell him, reaching toward the wall of cues. This time, I spare no thought and pick one on intuition. "I get the feeling you're going to be embarrassed enough…why make you wait and worry about it?"

The angel emits a petulant little laugh and shakes his head. I rack up the balls while Gabriel tells me, "You're awfully confident for somebody who lost last time."

"Just get your cue," I tell him, dropping the 8 into the rack.

Since he challenged me, I get the break. Our rematch is, at the start, an uncanny mirror image of our first game. I sink an even ball right away—but, as it rolls into the corner pocket, a sudden flow sweeps over me. There have been a few times in life where I'll enter a competition or see a job offer and just feel my destiny to win it is a simple matter of making the right moves.

This is all I feel now. Defeating the angel at this pool table is a given. Guaranteed so long as I enact the proper combination of shots. Like a ritual for my success: one played out only in that very moment, and customized only to me.

"You know," I tell Gabe as I sink a second ball, scan the table, then move to the far end across from him, "I have to confess that I lied to you, Gabriel."

"Oh?"

"Uh-huh. I think I told you I didn't come in on Wednesday because of car trouble…that was true in part, but it was more complicated than that."

I take a shot. My targeted 6-ball bounces right into the side pocket I called. "See…I actually got into a fight. At least, somebody picked a fight with me."

"You must have been very shaken up," says Gabriel with a notable lack of empathy. "Where did this happen?"

"While I was just walking down the street. I couldn't believe it…it was easier to call in." With a thunderous crack and a surge of adrenaline, I damn the 12 to the corner pit and continue prowling around the table. Beatrix is literally on the edge of her seat, lip bitten as she watches, the heel of her shoe hooked into the crossbar of her stool as though to keep her in place.

Gabe's hands tighten into pale fists as I assess the spread. No wonder he's nervous. After another shot, only the 10 and the 14 are left for me. It would be gentlemanly of me to miss the next shot and let him have at least a few tries, but I've never run a pool table so thoroughly before, and besides…gentlemen don't assault other gentlemen in the street. I have absolutely no interest in taking it easy on him, and I really have no interest in protecting his feelings.

"Whomever it was that attacked me, I didn't exactly leave him in a comfortable condition. Scraped himself up falling and got a nasty black eye or two from me—but I didn't see his face so I didn't get to see how bad it was." When the I drop my last ball into the corner pocket, I straighten up and look at him.

"When did you start wearing concealer, by the way?"

"It would be very easy for you to walk away from this table and act like nothing has happened, Legion," says Gabriel softly.

The game is over and both of us know it. I prolong the agony and start to sink his balls, each shot a perfect strike through his heart. Down goes the 11 after banking off the side as I say, "And let you keep the seal? No thanks."

"If you break the seal, I will have no choice but to engage you in combat. Think this through. Think of what it means."

"It means that when I'm through with you, there will be one less angel to stalk me in the street."

"No," he says quickly, his lips tense. "No—it means that there will be more angels coming for you, and more urgently. If you were to defeat me, many more would take up the cause in my stead or come around to avenge me."

While the disgraced 9 ball rolls with a cruelly meandering pace toward its end, I go ahead and shoot the 7. Both drop into their respective pockets at the same time. "Well, now…I'd love to say that the idea scares me, but Beatrix here just shared some interesting information about your seal."

I gesture toward her, realizing how uncannily quiet it has become outside of our conversation and the clacking of billiard balls into one another. While, following my eyes, he glances in the direction of the silent bartender, I snap the 3 and then the 5 off and out of sight. Saving the 1-ball for second to last, I tell him, "If these seals really work the way she says they do, and I'm really as all-powerful as everybody fears or hopes I am, then I get the feeling I might find humbling a load of immortal beings pretty damn fun."

I strike the chalk against the tip of my cue and bend to take the final shot. Beatrix cheers for me, clapping her hands while the 8-ball drops into the corner pocket and disappears—at least, until the next game is played upon the table.

As the ball thumps into its place, the seal appears in a brilliant silvery halo before us. Its characters, too many in number and too foreign for my eye to discern, swirl about the central symbol of the planet Mars. The light blazes brighter for a period of several seconds, peaking in what seems to be a literal explosion. I reflexively wince and raise my hands against the blast—and though there is no energy from the shattering of the seal that physically impacts me, the sudden burst of a great projectile of golden light knocks me back into the wall of the bar. My head is left ringing so sharply that I can't hear Beatrix call my name.

It's like being hit in the eyes and nose and mouth with a firecracker. The inside of my brain sparks with an agony that bounces between the neurons and races down my spine, and I grimace through it all. Smoke curls off my body as I struggle to see through the pain. Pushing myself back up to my feet with the help of the pool cue still clutched in my hands, I say, "I thought angels were bound by the physical laws of Earth."

THIS IS NOT EARTH

The voice rings in my head in a chorus that would surely terrify most men into immediate retreat, as even I have a flare of reticence to hear it. Different voices— some harmonious, some atonal, none human—put the words into my head amid a breath that howls like a gale. Beatrix cries out and shields her eyes, her own disguise stripped away by the presence of the angel unclothed between us.

So far as I can tell, the angel does not exist from the waist down. Its elongated black torso is set in a rich bed of energy that seems cloudlike, but which I know is not a cloud as we know it on Earth. Space and time warps around it, all reality twisting into its back to form the substance of its wings. Because of the way its movements cause space around it to skip and shift, I cannot seem to get a proper bead on its arms. Even its face eludes me like the material of the black stone I made yesterday.

And, amid these howling voices, this thing shoots across the bar at me.

I raise my cue to meet it, blocking its bare-handed swipe just in time.

For half a second, I'm surprised I'm able to make it; that the cue doesn't snap under the pressure.

Then, deciding there's no limit to what I'm capable of if all this is really happening to me, I push off against the angel and take my turn to lay a strike.

The angel is impossibly fast and meets me blow-for-blow, never letting me get a hit in against it—and though at first I'm discouraged, I quickly realize that I am going toe-to-toe with this archangel using nothing more than a pool cue. We beat one another back toward the entrance of the bar, the twitching angel sometimes skipping through space toward me and then back a little like an old film reel. While it gets lucky and pins me against the curiously stuck door of the establishment, I reach down with one hand to push it open and notice Frank frozen in motion, his gaze turned toward the corner of the bar and the site of our pool game. Only when I'm forced to step aside and duck a claw does the proprietor move toward the pool tables. When I stop, he stops.

A dimension where time and space truly *are* one and the same.

The uncountable mouths of the angel gnash their fangs. Finally they succeed in chomping the pool cue in half. Gritting my teeth, I toss the pieces down. "If this isn't Earth, then where are we?"

THIS IS NOT TIME

"No shit," I tell it, reaching behind me to blindly open the door and duck outside. As I hit the silent night, I curse myself for parking two blocks down and have to break into a sprint.

The angel blasts after me, its speed impossible to compensate for.

BE AFRAID
BE AFRAID
BE AFRAID
BE AFRAID

The howling in my soul makes a compelling argument, but I don't find myself afraid so much as annoyed that it would presume it could make me afraid.

After all…if that's what an angel like Gabe looks like, all I can do is wonder about myself.

Not to mention Beatrix.

"Master," she cries, jetting between us and sweeping me off in a direction I didn't know existed.

The angel, whose oily claws had been millimeters from rending my flesh along with the back of my shirt, disappears. Tucson's sounds of unsteady late-night traffic resume.

Setting me back on my feet and grabbing my hand to

run with me, Beatrix asks, "Are you all right?"

"Where were we just now?"

"A different spatial dimension," she explains. "A pocket of space that is free from the influence of Earth and physical laws. Eternity. From that condition of Earth, one can receive passage to celestial realms and dissolve into unity with the godhead—or, far more likely, be subject to annihilation by angels for seeing things that humans are not meant to see."

"Do demons dwell there, too?"

"No. I've never seen it before, but I knew it at once when I saw it. I was wondering why nobody from the other side of the bar had anything to say about the noise—"

I have many more questions, but Beatrix abruptly yelps. Her hand is yanked from mine and she disappears with a cry: a shortened scream infinitely more chilling than a completed one.

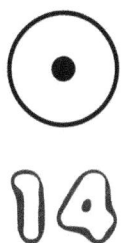

14

TO SAY BEATRIX disappeared gives the wrong impression. In fact, it's more as though she were pulled off-stage in some direction that I didn't realize existed. A secret cardinal direction whose existence is now sensible and obvious to me but which nonetheless remains invisible to my human eye.

Pumping my limbs as fast as I can, I focus on getting to the car and retrieving the gun. The sidewalk rattles near me. I duck into the parking lot adjacent just as a newspaper box shatters in an explosion of twisted metal, broken plastic and fresh confetti.

My brow sweats a little, I admit it…but not nearly as much as when I see my car ahead of me, illuminated in its corner spot by a street light that perfectly demonstrates the steady cracking of the asphalt in the Lincoln's direction. I swear, trying to pick up the pace.

Too late. My heart breaks: the trunk crumples, the hood snaps, and the entire frame twists as though trampled by a parade of invisible elephants.

"My fucking car!"

I scream in true horror, more upset about the vehicle in that second than I am about the gun. Whipping my head around, I try again to find some secret entrance to this other place. Once again I fail. The asphalt cracks anew, this time toward me, and I'm wondering how to fight an opponent I can't see when the squeal of tires announces my lady in shining armor.

"Get in," Despina screams while great potholes snap in the parking lot all of ten feet from us.

I've got one foot in when she's already hitting the gas, but that's all I need. Leaving the door open and propping the other foot upon the frame of the vehicle, I hang onto the side and tell her, "I need something from the car."

"Do you think you can get it open?"

"I'm going to have to climb in through a window."

While Despina looks at me in grim displeasure, I notice the gleaming black stone in her car's cupholder. She whips the car back around, the door unsteady in my hand. The stone's nearness recalls the hideous visage of the angel, its entire being unsuited for even my humanoid gaze. As though its very body were made of the material of that other, impossible dimension.

Following the call of that increasingly fruitful intuition, I duck down into the car only to grab the stone.

"*Really,*" Despina remarks while her vehicle skids to a halt beside the ruins of mine.

"Hey, you don't know how my mother is going to be if I forget this thing…"

As, on the other side of the parking lot, our pursuer re-orients itself and makes its fast way toward us, I leap down upon the asphalt. Using the hard little stone, I smash the already spiderwebbed window and reach in to force the handle of the deformed door. It grinds open as the ground rattles with the nearness of the angel. My girlfriend tells me, "Hurry! Hurry! *Rapidamente!*"

Teeth clenched, I jam my hand under the crunched seat, scrape my wrist open on a jagged piece of metal, and struggle to contort the gun from its hiding place.

The already crumbled blacktop beneath the tailgate scatters with an invisible step.

"Legion," screams Despina.

With a good yank, I jerk the gun free of the car, raise it, and fire an indigo shot in the direction of the invisible assailant.

A hideous noise raises in my skull. Despina hears it too and takes it a lot worse, her eyes widening and her hands flying to her ears. "What was that?"

"Get out of here," I tell her, shutting her door. End of conversation. This is my fight: having her here will only endanger her.

Though she looks reluctant, she obeys me. The car snarls off while the parking lot thunders with a new, faster set of steps.

The glowing gun still raised, I fire off six rounds and am amazed to find the weapon shows no sign of requiring so much as a cool-down period, let alone ammunition. As the angel howls in my soul and its approach is put on pause, I look down at the stone in my hand.

If there's a way for my humanoid body to access that other dimension without breaking a seal or accessing my true form, I get the feeling this stone is it. But how?

There's little time to ponder. A long trail of asphalt shattered by the angel's energy jerks into motion and dashes away. A streetlight at the edge of the lot careens toward me. When I duck to the side and get my bearings again, the angel is coming toward me at a faster pace than ever.

Panicking, I hurl the stone in hopes of fending it off or making it wince, thereby earning enough time to unload as many shots as this gun can produce.

I get off three before the stone, struck midair by an indigo projectile, explodes in a great cloud of darkness that reveals the angel charging through that other dimension of hidden space, which expands in a tremendous cloud that consumes me. Reality is once more subject to the strange energy patterns that become most apparent near the angel's back, and at least I am able to see Beatrix collapsed on the ground at the parking lot's entrance.

Calling her name and finding her utterly still, I grit my teeth and return my attention to the angel. The stone—in one piece again, strangely—rolls to its feet and goes ignored amid its howls of rage and agony. Blood in colors I've never perceived oozes from wounds that seem to be burns as much as bullet holes, each one of its many mouths wailing in heinous agony while I gawk. The so-called cloud in which its torso is poised now drags along the ground, and though it pulls itself along with its twitching arms, it remains as fast as anything I have ever seen outside of cars and nature documentaries.

YOU ARE DAMNED

"If angels like you are what people see when they're saved, I don't think I want to be anything *but* damned. Did you kill Beatrix?"

SHE IS NOTHING
SHE IS THE SLAVE OF A SLAVE
SHE IS THE THOUGHT OF A TRAITOR
YOU WILL DIE

One claw raises to swipe at me, then another. Rage fills me to the brim to find the angel will not stop—that it is a remorseless creature of death and destruction without the least regard for Beatrix, like an automaton made only to kill.

"No," I tell it while raising my arm to block its blow. "You're the only dead one here."

My black-clawed hand catches the twisted digits of the angel. All its voices scream to look upon me.

Almost surprised, I glance down at myself. Then, second by second, I remember. Yes! Oh, yes. Of course. Blessed Beatrix, waking me up. For these sweet seconds, I am my true self, and I can even almost remember my name.

I have missed this body.

In its efforts to free itself from my clutches, the screaming angel yanks and yanks until the gray flesh of its arm is degloved in my grip. Only when its muscles slip from its flesh does it manage to free itself from me. While it goes writhing off into the sky like a wounded fish fleeing from the jaws of a shark through the dark ocean brine, I launch off and follow it. As I do, my preferred mouth consumes the flesh-trophy I have acquired.

YOU WILL BE PUNISHED

I do not speak to tell it I have already been punished. Though it raises many energy barriers with the last of its strength, I split right through them and catch hold of the angel's wings.

It screams. I tear reality from the middle of its back and send it falling down to the ground, where it lands with a great cracking of bones and splattering of blood.

Inhaling, exhaling, feeling myself as truly the center of

existence's tapestry, I gently alight beside the wheezing beast. Gabriel's eyes roll listlessly toward me as I cross to the parking lot, retrieve the stone I remember now is called an angel's eye, and return to my broken opponent.

Now my voices are the ones that roar between our souls.

ALL THEY THAT TAKE THE SWORD SHALL PERISH BY THE SWORD

Spittle tainted with angel blood drools from my fangs as I bend over him, crushing the stone for a second and final time. As the soul is annihilated in my hand, light bursts across my eyes and reality flips right-side out again.

Gabe lays beneath me on his back, looking absolutely stunned. My hand is empty. It is also humanoid again.

Knowing he will never be an angel again, I straighten up and slide the gun into my belt.

"Maybe living as a mortal and dying a human death will teach you a little empathy."

He looks so dazed that I'm not even sure he's heard me—or, for that matter, that he knows anything about what has happened between us. Does he remember that he's an angel, or was? Does he remember me as anything other than a vaguely lazy employee?

Maybe someday all this will come to him in dreams… or upon the hour of the divine union these angels would destroy the world to achieve.

Leaving him behind to sort himself out, I cross the parking lot and stoop to cradle Beatrix in my arms. Her body is limp and her breathing is shallow but, like Gabe, she appears absolutely unharmed. Maybe in that other place things would be different, but here, she just looks as though she's fainted.

Without the least regard for our location or the sounds of sirens in the distance, I lower my head and press a long, lingering kiss to Beatrix's relaxed lips. My mind focuses on the sweetness of her tongue and the yearning she inspires in my body, dredging up vivid images of her eagerness to please me. As my tongue slides in against hers, I trail my hand over her waist and up along her breast.

Softly, as though rousing from sleep, Beatrix moans. Her lips gradually work to return the kiss. Soon— breathless, flushed, and horny as ever—she writhes in my embrace and stirs fully awake with a gasp like someone coming out of a nightmare. I draw back from our kiss, relief sweeping over me.

"Master!" Clutching my shirt, she begs to know, "Master, are you all right?"

Emotion swells in my heart: I hold her tightly to my chest and lower my cheek to the top of her head.

We have to leave right this very instant, at least once she's gathered her strength enough to fix the car...but I am never too rushed to appreciate being alive.

EPILOGUE

GABE SHAKES MY hand before passing me the cardboard box that's been on his desk for the duration of our conversation.

"Well," he summarizes with a sigh and a shake of his head, "I'm sorry to see you leave my department, but I really do think you'll be a lot more satisfied with this change."

"I think I will, too."

"Don't be a stranger!" As he gets the door for me, one hand upon my shoulder, he pats me and says, "Hope I'll see you at the company Christmas party come the end of the year."

I assure him he will. When his door is shut, I make my way back past Beatrix's desk with my heart as light as a feather. She pouts playfully at me, leaning forward to flash me a glance down her blouse. "You're really leaving us, Mr. Legion?"

"I'm afraid so, Beatrix…this floor, anyway. But I'm sure we'll see each other around, here and there. Maybe we could get a coffee sometime."

"I'd like that," she says with a cheeky little grin, returning to her pantomime of office work amid stacks of files and dubious paperwork. "Good luck in sales, sir."

"Thanks, Beatrix…break a leg down here."

Around the corner, back in my cubicle, I gather the miniscule assortment of personal possessions I have bothered to place around the depressing gray walls. Notes I will only throw away once I've had time to sort through the box, a tiny bonsai plant that my mother bought me from some kit and clings to life by sheer luck, a new angel's eye stone that I made and decided to start keeping at work just in case.

While I pack, Mike appears in the cube doorway with a sad look on his face.

"So the day's come after all…I was hoping it would take a little while before they worked out your transfer."

"I thought it would, but I guess they're really desperate for new blood up there." Shaking my head, I toss the rest of the papers pinned to my walls into the garbage can. Meanwhile my brain intones the schoolboy's rhyme: *No more classes, no more books, no more teachers' dirty looks.* "I have to admit, I'm not too sad that they got it together by the end of the day, but I'll definitely be sorry to not sit by you. You should get yourself transferred up with me, we'd be a great team."

"Me? Nah…I'm not a "people" person. More of a "sit in a cubicle and work on projects in peace" person. Still—lunch once a week?"

"More, if we can," I say, shaking hands, then turning it into an embrace. Patting his shoulder to punctuate the gesture, I add, "Thanks for making life down here more bearable, Mike."

"Ah, shucks! You'll choke me up...go get 'em, tiger."

At his light punch, he ducks into his cube and leaves me alone. I grin to myself and turn back to resume tidying, but I discover with a pang of strange sorrow that I've finished. Amazingly, it's all already done.

Somehow, I feel almost sorry. Here's a chapter of my life behind me. The final cubicle in which I sat, doing the final job I would ever do in total human ignorance of my own secret condition. Of my own true nature, which follows me to the gleaming elevator doors.

It has been a long weekend. I have thought many times about quitting Helcom altogether, but Beatrix was right to persuade me to stay. Since breaking through with the angel tear and seeing my true self for the first time in an eternity, I have felt a new indignation. A little taste of memory, a little whisper of old lost power, and I am now permanently insulted that these fools have had the audacity to do such a thing to me.

Me.

The best and brightest of the angels.

The only ones who deserve punishment is them— all those once involved in establishing and maintaining this charade. Especially those closest to home, all those keeping me distracted with the regulations and workflow of Helcom.

So, because they pushed me into it, I have made my decision.

First, I'm going to do whatever it takes to get to the top of Helcom.

Then, I'm going to evict every last angel from this

planet. However long it takes, I'm going to liberate Earth from its threat of annihilation and its constant cloak of unconscious control mechanisms. I'm going to exorcise it of its overlords and let it have true free will.

After all…if Baphomet—a dream, a thought, a creation of my own mind and will and power—can exhibit such a rich inner life, can be loving and kind and experience a sense of self and emotion and existence, then I don't see why the same isn't true of very single being on this thinly disguised prison ship. I don't see why a single one of them should have to suffer or die, ever—let alone because of me.

The angels are demented. That much is clear.

Sort of makes me worry about their boss.

The doors slide open to the sales floor, four above ours, and I run nearly face-first into a woman trying to board the elevator. Her dark eyes widen behind her wire-frame glasses, her mouth shaping into an 'o' of surprise. As we both produce the same automatic word—"Sorry!"—despite the lack of collision, we take in one another's features. Her cheeks, framed by the short black curtain of her bob hairdo, turn candy apple red in a fraction of a second.

"Oh," she says in a smooth voice while stepping back. She glances down at the box in my hands and then back up to my face. "Oh, excuse me—are you a new hire?"

"Transferred," I say, getting the sense that she enjoys having my eyes on her. While I step out of the elevator but keep my foot against one of the doors to leave it open, I let her see all the places I look in the space of a few precious seconds—slim, tight, pert, cute, everything nicely accented in a white blouse with a black sailor knot tie and a black pencil skirt that falls to her knees, squeezing her thighs the way my hands itch to. When my eyes lift again to her face, she smiles in a coy way.

"Well, I'm sure they must think you'll be a good fit."

"Most people find that I am," I tell her, shifting the box in my arms against one hip to offer my hand. "Vic Legion."

She smiles, the hint of a lip-bite dancing about its very edge as she slides her hand into mine. Is it my imagination, or are those goosebumps rising along her neck? After a quick shake, she slips past me and into the elevator.

"You can call me "Gretchen,"" she says. While I try to remember where I've heard the name, I remove my foot from the door. Her smile widens.

A genuine fang glints beside the point of her cuspid. Both gleam at me as the doors slide shut.

"Nice to meet you, Master."

My jaw falls open. Before I can get out the words, "What—hey," the elevator doors shut.

Annoyed, I grit my teeth. Could I beat her to the first floor by taking the stairs? Where are they?

"Aha, there you are! Mr. Legion!"

From across the warehouse-sized floor of open desks, ringing telephones and even less privacy than was available amid the engineers, my new boss flashes a winning smile and extricates himself from his conversation. Coming toward me with a jocular shake of the hand that sadly erases the sensory appreciation inspired by Gretchen, Raphael slides an arm around my shoulders. He smells like Old Spice and mothballs. I feel he is almost certainly an angel.

"I was so glad to see your e-mail this morning! Thank you for coming up on short notice. We're delighted to have you aboard."

"The pleasure's all mine."

His well-groomed white beard competes for purity with the flash of his dentures as he beams with approval. "That's the spirit! Now, my boy, I'm actually due to leave in a few minutes, so why don't we have a short orientation and worry about the rest tomorrow? You can take the rest of the day off too, if you'd like. Don't think either one of us will be getting anything meaningful done between now and four."

"That's one way to get off on the right foot with a new transfer."

Raphael laughs again, opening the door to his office along the western wall. "Oh yes, Mr. Legion, I think you'll like it quite a bit more up here in sales…we're much, much more relaxed."

I'll believe it when I see it.

The orientation is extremely short and basically consists of Raphael handing me a product guide, assigning me a few videos to watch at my desk over the next two workdays, and telling me I'll be assigned a salesperson to shadow sometime tomorrow. I already have a good guess as to who that will be…even if she has to claw somebody's eyes out to get the assignment.

Then, when it's all over, Raphael shows me to a desk at the edge of the floor (too close to his office for my liking), tells me he'll get IT to set me up on the salesforce database, and takes a hat down from the hook behind his office door. After telling me again that he's glad I'm aboard, he departs.

I look at my watch, wait all of sixty seconds, and follow suit.

Normally I'd be more gracious and stick around five or ten minutes to set up my desk a bit and introduce myself to people around, but I'm a bit occupied. I've been looking forward to tonight for almost a week, and my body is on fire as I make my way to the once more resurrected Lincoln—whose abuse, I sense, is only beginning. Poor car…immortality isn't all it's cracked up to be in some ways.

In other ways, though, it's a pretty sweet gig. This whole thing, me as a demon lord…sure, maybe it's a little surprising. Yet, thinking of all the good things it's already brought to me, who could complain? I'm home by one, where I shower, put on fresh clothes, and later apply a spritz of cologne. Then, when Beatrice is back from work and likewise freshened up, we cross the hall and knock on Melody's door.

*   *   *

After dinner, Melody serves chocolate-dipped strawberries while Beatrix and I canoodle on the couch that seems to have good energy for inspiring bad behavior. "I still can't believe you tried to tell me you two were brother and sister," says Melody with a laugh, shaking her head and sliding into the corner cushion. While I pluck a fruit from the tray on the coffee table, Beatrix giggles evilly.

"I wish! That sounds sort of hot."

"You watch too much porn," I tell Beatrix, pressing the strawberry to her lips. "Not that you need to…I try to keep you busy."

Leaning back against my chest, half in my lap already, the disguised succubus goes on after swallowing. "I don't have to watch porn at all—I just think it's hot to be naughty." Smiling, reaching back behind her to caress my face, Beatrix gazes at our blushing hostess and says, "You like to be naughty, don't you, Melody?"

"Well—"

"You don't have to fib," says Beatrix, provocatively writhing a bit more emphatically into my lap. The little red dress she's worn to match her nails rides up her tanned thighs—not quite high enough to show her panties, but almost. My dick has been leaping to attention at the lightest stimulus all day. Certainly once we arrived at Melody's apartment for our dinner date. Her face and lips flushed with similar anticipation, Beatrix gazes at Melody while stroking her nails up over my scalp. "We're both very naughty…at least, I am."

Beatrix's blonde head tips back toward me, her lips parted to plead for a kiss. I oblige her, sliding my hand around the column of her throat and bending to trail my tongue into her mouth. As she softly moans, I watch Melody from the corner of my eye. Though she looks so bashful she seems poised to glance away already, our hostess is nonetheless transfixed by the image of our embrace. As my hand slides down over Beatrix's breast, my fingers naturally finding her stiffening nipple through the fabric, Melody produces a noise like a soft gasp. Her fingers tighten in the floral pattern of her sun dress.

"Oh," moans Beatrix while I tickle around her areola and sometimes roll the peak between my thumb and forefinger, "I love it when Master touches me…but I especially love it when someone watches him touch me…"

Her blush deepening, a certain look of shock touching her face, Melody says, "So you *do* call him 'Master…' I thought I was hearing things."

"Oh, no," I say, sliding my hand down Beatrix's waist while she moans in frustration, "Beatrix is my happy little sex slave. Aren't you, slut?"

"Yes, sir, yes, Master! Oh…" Moaning while I draw high her skirt to display her black lace panties and garters to Melody, Beatrix writhes and reaches back to fondle my cock through my trousers. "Fuck, oh, sir! You make me such a horny little bitch."

With her displayed, I slide my hand back up to tease her other breast now. Melody watches, lips parted, face red with desire. "No wonder Melody loves to listen to you getting fucked…who doesn't love to listen to a horny little bitch who loves it? I'll bet your pussy is wet already, huh."

"Yes, sir! Oh, I'm all ready for you."

I chuckle, looking expectantly over at Melody. "She's like this at all hours…maybe once you get used to her, you can help me wear her out sometimes. You're so beautiful, Melody." Her blush deepens to hear such a thing and, as she bites her lip, I tell her, "Come here."

Still with her teeth sunken into that plump lip, Melody glances at Beatrix. Then, leaning toward us, she pauses before coming to us.

Incredibly, my innocent neighbor's first kiss of the night is for my moaning concubine. I exhale while Melody takes the demon's face in her soft hands and presses mouth to mouth. Beatrix groans, receiving our neighbor's tongue and sliding a hand over her bosom. While, gasping at the contact, Melody briefly pulls away, she quickly leans back in for another kiss.

Then, she leans past, to me.

I catch her face in my hand and let my fingers drift back around to fit into her silvery hair. The careful up-do into which she's put it is immediately spoiled, but she doesn't comment if she cares at all. She only gazes into my face with lust, letting me draw her close against Beatrix's body and kiss her tender mouth. Melody's shy lips open to me, the gasps of her tongue awash with bliss as I pillage the chamber of her throat. She groans, her body lightly grinding against Beatrix's.

When we part for breath, the girls are making out again. I slide my hand down Beatrix's waist and this time run my fingers over the crotch of her panties.

The lace of the g-string is absolutely soaked through. My cock twitches at the sound of her whimper. When Melody leans back from the kiss, she glances down at the caressing with a moan.

Regarding her through heavily lidded eyes, I ask Melody, "You like to watch as much as you like to listen, huh? You're probably pretty wet, yourself."

Gasping, Melody looks bashfully at me and confesses, "I've been wet all night."

"Me, too," moans my slave, gazing up into my face with wanton lust. "Oh, sir, me, too…"

"What a horny couple of girls you are…I'm going to have to work hard to keep you two out of trouble. Let's see how wet your cute little pussy is, Melody…oh, Beatrix, I can't wait for you to see her."

While my demoness moans, Melody stutters out a shy gasp—a soft sort of laugh. "Now? Just like that?"

"No time like the present," I say with an encouraging grin, bending my head to kiss Beatrix. By the time our tongues have come untangled I've pushed her tiny little g-string to the side. "See? Look how nice and slutty and wet my slave is. Look how much she loves showing you."

In fact, Beatrix spreads her legs to assist me in my demonstration. Girl-cum oozes down her swollen folds and leaves her looking exceptionally desperate for a good, hard dicking tonight. While I tease her clit with the tip of one finger, she whines desperately and arches against my touch.

With a moan for the sight, Melody at last looks into my face with a mingling of determination and desire reflected in her own. Slowly, reaching up under the knee-length hem of her dress without showing anything, she pulls off her panties and slides them down her legs like a bride having her garter removed. When her white silk undies lay on the floor, innocent-looking Melody blushes that sweet scarlet hue I love to see and slowly draws her hem up her splayed legs. With one foot propped upon the couch and the other resting on the floor beside us, she reveals herself to me and the demoness I fondle.

"Oh, Melody!" I gasp with pleasure, my eyes surely all the brighter to see her labia parted by the intensity of her arousal—to my delight, permitting the sloppy leak of her lustful nectar. Removing my fingers from their petting of Beatrix, I reach across the couch and just barely tease the visible pink of Melody's clit peeking between her lips. She gasps, moaning, spreading her legs a little more.

"Come closer, baby," I tell her, pleased when she obeys with her gorgeous valley still on display. Soon her leg slides against Beatrix's, the girls half a cushion apart.

Looking into the innocent girl's eyes, I part her labia to let Beatrix take an appreciative look. "You like it when I tease your pussy in front of my fuck-slave, huh, sweetheart?"

Melody's lips fall open in shock as my finger brushes back and forth, sliding over her soaked clit with the greatest of ease. "Yes," she whispers, "yes, oh, it feels so dirty and good…oh, oh, mm—oh—"

"Can you believe she'd never even touched herself before this week?"

I ask this of Beatrix, who gasps in shock.

"What? Poor baby! Still learning about her body…oh, Master—may I teach her?"

With a groan at the thought, I make eye contact with Melody while sliding a finger into Beatrix's drenched pussy. The demon moans to be finger-fucked in front of the human, slowly massaging her own breasts and gazing at our friend.

"I don't know, baby," I tell Beatrix. "I was thinking of making you watch while I fucked her…I don't know if I want you cumming tonight."

With a low whine, a look of absolute delight contorting her face, Beatrix moans and says, "Oh, but Master, I'm a good girl! Oh, yes, I can be a good, agreeable little slave-girl! I promise not to cum! I want to watch you fuck Melody, but I also want to help her learn. May I, please, may I?"

"Hm…all right." I generously slide my fingers from her pussy amid a new flood of desire. "But if you cum by accident, I think I'm going to have to give you a spanking in front of Melody. And won't that embarrass you both?"

"I promise I'll be good," swears my slut, looking adoringly at Melody. "Have you looked at your pretty pussy a lot, Melody?"

Her eyes hazy with desire, her face bright with shame, Melody shakes her head. A few wisps of pale lilac hair swing around her face.

"That's okay," Beatrix says, sliding out of my lap a bit and a few inches closer to our hostess, both still on display. "It's all nice to touch, really…from your clit"— the succubus's red nail tickles the same mound of pink flesh that so entrances me and makes Melody almost scream with immediate overstimulation—"to your cunt. Did Master really take your virginity the other day?"

At Melody's shy nod, Beatrix's grin widens. The tip of her finger just teasing Melody's tight hole, she croons, "How fucking hot…I wish I had seen it, oh, a cute little virgin, mm…"

Moaning at the thought, Beatrix teases her finger

deeper before spreading the resulting cum all over Melody's clit. Now Melody openly moans and the succubus grins, asking, "You like that, huh, baby? Like being all naughty and dripping wet...I like it, too...."

Briefly contorting her legs, Beatrix slides her g-string away and lets it rest on the floor beside Melody's underwear. The demoness then spreads her legs again, her pussy lips swollen. She catches Mel's hand and guides it down. "Feel how soaked I am?"

Melody moans, nodding, and experimentally toys with Beatrix's clit before trailing along the lines of her beautiful, bare folds. "Oh," moans Melody, breathless with excitement as the succubus responds in kind, "oh, God, you're dripping wet...oh, you feel so soft..."

"So do you," says Beatrix, her purring voice husky with desire and delight. She leans forward then, her mouth stealing a kiss from Melody's barely ready lips.

While the girls pet each other, my prick throbs so viscerally I can't stand it anymore. As soft, feminine moans rise in harmony through the apartment, I slowly stroke my dick to the sight and marvel at the abandon they show for caressing one another. Melody really comes out of her shell with two people encouraging her. I finally see the importance of female role models for women.

"You sure do get sensitive when you're all soaked," says Beatrix with a giggle. "Oh, fuck...when I get wet like this, all I want is to get wetter and wetter...that's what's nice about two women being together...see..."

At last closing that ever-decreasing distance, Beatrix slides her naked, soaking pussy against Melody's swollen one. Both girls gasp, but especially Melody. Her toes curling, her brow furrowing, she looks past at the leisurely strokes I give my cock to the sight. She releases a long, low moan of desire.

While their clits rub together and their labia spread against one another, the sultry sound of slippery flesh keeps an audible tempo of their lust. Beatrix leans back against me, forcefully grinding her pussy against Melody's. Still moaning as though in a kind of amazement, Melody mirrors her, gazing at me with heat in her eyes while she and my sex slave flood each other's pussies.

"Oh, fuck!"

Beatrix moans while I let my free hand slide back to undo her dress's zipper and free her breasts from their confines. As her pink nipples burst from the fabric straining to maintain them, I groan and pick one to squeeze. The succubus's red mouth opens and, teeth briefly clenching with desire, she looks back down to more deliberately work her clitoris against Melody's. Our hostess nearly yelps, her eyelids fluttering at the sensation, shimmering strands of pleasure conjoining them when their labia briefly part. There's not the slightest hint of friction. Only of flowing pleasure as the girls slip back and forth: folds caressing folds; cunts oozing crystalline cum against each other; soft, bare labia kissing between locked thighs.

Those moments of their parting that let me see strings of shared cum are fewer and further between all the time, though. As they move faster, their bodies draw closer; their legs, more tightly tangled. Shining lust overflows from each woman's vulva and leaves the lucky light glinting off their flesh. I bend my head to kiss Beatrix.

When I do, Melody cries out amid the sudden tensing of her body.

"Oh," moans the demoness at the sight, licking her lips, "oh, yes! Isn't that *nice*, how's that feel? Cum for us, you little slut—oh, oh—oh, no—"

Beatrix's voice raises in a whimper and her eyes lock

onto mine. As her body trembles against me and Melody, I grin.

"I thought I told you no cumming tonight, bad girl."

"Mm, oh, fuck, Master!" Her back arching, her pussy grinding against the slick of Melody's, Beatrix groans and pets my face. "Master, oh, I'm sorry, I'm very sorry—"

"Come here, you disobedient little whore…"

Drawing Beatrix back from Melody, I yank her over stomach-down across my lap. While my slave groans to be so exposed, I land a quick slap on her upper thighs. Then another across her rear, and another. "What a bad girl you are," I tell her, glancing at Melody from the corner of my eye to see she watches, riveted, her face full of dreams and her fingers just beginning to work between her own thighs. "I knew you were going to sneak out an orgasm…now I really have no choice but to make you watch me fuck Melody."

My spanks pay special—and especially sharp— attention to Beatrix's pouty labia, which makes her scream with absolute ecstasy. While I spank her pussy, she whimpers, "Oh, Master, but I'm just so horny! I need to cum all the time, ah—"

As she yelps at a particularly hard spank, I grind my cock against her thigh. "You need to learn some self-control. I don't even want to see you touch yourself, slave."

With another, brisk bursts of spanks, I bring Beatrix close to what I sense is another orgasm that I narrowly avoid when I lift my hand away. While the demoness emits a miserable moan of frustration, I push her from my lap and turn to Melody. She freezes, a gasp on her lips, fright in her eyes as if she's forgotten she exists until just now.

"Sorry about Beatrix," I tell her, drawing her into my arms and gazing admiringly down at the masturbation she's paused. As I bend my head to kiss her supple mouth, her damp fingertips curl around my exposed prick.

Slowly, experimentally, they trail all around it. After encouraging her with a few avid plunges of my tongue, I tell her, "How about you and I go make ourselves more comfortable in your bed, baby?"

Biting her lip, glancing only briefly at Beatrix—watching us with eager, undisguised lust—Melody nods. I pick her up, her slight weight almost effortless to carry bridal-style into her room. She gasps, slinging her arms around my neck, while Beatrix moans to crawl after us and shut the door so we don't have to.

I lay lovely Melody down on the bed and, between kisses, undress her. The succubus slithers up behind me and slowly unbuckles my belt. After drawing my trousers and boxers down to properly free my cock, Beatrix strokes it with longing. At the same time, she moans to admire Melody's exposed pussy.

"I can't believe I'm doing this," whispers Melody, gasping as I pull her dress over her head and leave her lying there totally naked. Her eyes focus on my dick—and Beatrix's steadily pumping hand. "You really don't mind?"

"Of course not…" Beatrix moans, almost touching herself with her free hand and, groaning in frustration, instead lifting it to tangle her fingers in her hair. "Oh, of course not, no…I want to see Master fuck as many women as he wants to fuck, and help him whenever he'll let me. Oh, Melody! And I *really* want to see him fuck your cute pussy…still so wet…fuck, I'm still so wet. Master, oh, you're being so mean…"

"You deserve it for disobeying me, slut. Now get on the bed and watch…and keep your hands where I can see them."

While, groaning, Beatrix releases me to obey, Melody bites her lip and glances down at the member I rest between her legs. She reaches out and draws me close, stroking me in emulation of Beatrix's confident grip with one hand lifting to my chest. As I push into the hallowed embrace of her gorgeous body, she shudders and kisses me with a fierceness equal to that of Beatrix.

"Ah!" Her brow furrowing while I groan at the hypertense squeeze around me, Melody takes my cock even more eagerly than she did the first time. She's even wetter, too, which I can't help but attribute to Beatrix's presence—and observation. While I slowly ease my cock deeper and deeper into Melody's overflowing pussy, Beatrix moans at the sight and leans down to kiss the corner of Melody's mouth.

"Oh, fuck, look at that! Isn't Master's cock the best? So big and hard. It looks like it fills you up very nicely…" Smiling, Beatrix slides her hand over Melody's breast, then down further. Melody groans while Beatrix toys with her clitoris, a sight that makes me fuck her just a little harder. Still practically a virgin, Melody whimpers, then lets it all out in a moan of bliss that seems to emulate the flood of her pussy. Beatrix's eyes sparkle as she exclaims, "Oh, Melody! I love playing with your cute little clit…oh…"

Whining, looking at me with desperation in her eyes, Beatrix then wiggles her own thighs together. "That looks so fucking good. I wish Master would let me touch myself…"

"You already had your chance to cum, slave, even though I told you not to. Now you just get to watch… good girl for helping, though. Ah, fuck, that's right, get Melody nice and extra wet for me."

Melody seems to be barely containing a scream as

I pound into her, shifting her hips up a little to really ram into the g-spot already swollen with ecstasy. She trembles as Beatrix picks up the pace of her teasing, and while her soaked channel squeezes around me, her legs wrap around my body.

Then, something beautiful and incredibly hot happens.

As she peaks in her orgasm, Melody cries out, "Oh! Oh, God, oh, yes! Ah—ah—Master—"

I groan, and so does my sexy demon fuck-slave. "You want to be my slave, too, do you, Melody?"

"O—oh! Oh, no, I—"

But her words dissolve in a low keen as I fuck her harder, my voice almost tender as I murmur to her.

"It's all right, you don't have to be shy…I can be your master, too, baby, ah! I know you want it…I know you want to be my little slave just like Beatrix…just like Despina…I'll introduce you all sometime, ah, fuck, you girls can play together."

While my fingers sink into her hip, Melody's back arches. At last, she unleashes a scream. Her nearly shocked eyes stare up into mine as I tell her, "Just tell me you want to call me 'Master,' baby…tell me you want to be my slave."

"Oh—oh—I want to be your slave," repeats Melody in a whine so sexy I could almost explode. "Please! I want to call you 'Master,' too, and—oh, oh! I want to know what it's like to be—spanked."

She can barely say the word, but Beatrix moans like she screamed it.

"It's so fun…I especially love it when Master spanks my pussy…oh, you'll love being Master's slave with me!"

"Please, oh"—Melody's pure, innocent eyes find mine. She begs while pawing at my chest—"please, sir! Will you be my master, too?"

I groan, hammering into her, assuring her, "Oh, yeah, baby, of course, of course…my good little slave, you can call me whatever you want."

"Master," she screams then as I stroke her g-spot in a wild, relentless rhythm. "Oh, Master! Master, Master, yes! Legion!"

Between my fucking and Beatrix's fondling, Melody cums in a rapid explosion of contorting muscles. I sigh her name, admiring her, then lean down to kiss her and Beatrix in turn. "But you know…"

I press my mouth to the corner of her lips and then to the ridge of her ear. While slowly, agonizingly sliding my cock out of her, I murmur to Melody, "Sometimes slave-girls have to watch their master fuck other slave-girls… and not slave-girls. So you might have to watch me just like Beatrix here is. But it makes you wet to be jealous, huh?"

Moaning, nodding as her orgasm slowly recedes to leave her hornier than ever, Melody whispers, "Yes, sir, yes…oh, I want to be jealous…I want to see you fuck Beatrix…"

"Well, Beatrix…sounds like it's your lucky day. Remember, though…"

While I turn her over on hands and knees and position myself behind her drooling pussy, sparkling-eyed Beatrix moans with anticipation, delight, frustration. "I can't even cum *now?*"

"You don't deserve it, slut," I tell her, gripping her thick head of hair to use those golden locks like reins. With my other hand, I slide into a pussy so eager that her girl-cum spurts out around me. I groan, slowly beginning to fuck her while, beside us, Melody gasps at the sight. Chuckling, I tell her, "Oh, and *what* a slut…both so wet…you girls like rubbing pussies, don't you…"

"Mm! Yes, yes, Master!" Beatrix screams, her head thrust back while I throw myself into pounding her as roughly as I know she needs. "Oh, Master, yes, Melody has such a pretty, pretty pussy!"

"Glad you like it…let Master watch Beatrix lick that pretty pussy of yours, Melody."

Gasping, then groaning with delight, Melody looks shy for only a second before sliding around and offering her spread legs to Beatrix. I sigh to see how avidly the demoness throws herself into it, sliding her arms around Melody's legs and covering her shining puss with kisses. While Melody gasps from the first contact, I grip Beatrix's hips and pound her hard enough to bruise. The demoness groans, her toes curling, her fingers reverently spreading Melody's labia to lick her pussy clean.

"Fuck, ah, doesn't that feel good, Melody…ah, baby…" Beatrix's cunt engulfs me in such a sea of bliss that I momentarily forget the vision before me and become focused on the woman I'm inside. I reach down, kissing the back of her neck and massaging her breasts while I fuck her with every intent to make her orgasm against her will. She moans, panting against Melody's pussy while I kiss my demon-girl's ear.

"What a beautiful pussy you have, Beatrix, baby… oh, fuck, ah, just made for your master's cock, baby, ah, fuck…"

Hearing me speak to Beatrix this way makes Melody moan, another climax clearly rising in her at a fast rate. "Oh," she whimpers, "oh, God, I don't know why this makes me so excited, ah! Oh, Beatrix, that feels so good…"

"That's good, baby, oh, that's good…oh, let Master watch you cum. Don't you want to see your new slave cum, sir?"

"Of course I do, because she's a good girl who deserves it…not like you, you dirty fucking slut." While I pound Beatrix harder, her body practically vibrating with a bliss she struggles to keep from mounting to orgasm, I pinch her nipple and tell her sternly, "Make my new favorite slave cum for me, bitch."

"Oh, sir! Oh, um, yes, Master, right away, uh—oh—oh—"

Beatrix looks pained as she struggles against the orgasm, her tongue working rapidly against her new friend's pussy while I hold her head down with one hand. Seeing and hearing all of this, Melody looks shocked, but a few seconds later she is wracked with an orgasm so incredible that I swear I can feel it like one of my own. Beatrix and I both gasp, riveted as Melody screams at a pitch high enough to snap glass.

"Legion," she screams, "oh, Master! Oh, Legion! Yes, yes, oh, yes! I want to serve you forever!"

My orgasm rushing upon me, my mind whirring to wonder how eagerly Melody will lick my creampie out of Beatrix's pussy, I am so stunned by the sudden burst of light emanating from Melody's heart that I feel as if a camera has flashed in my field of vision. Copper: the Seal of Venus.

That's one way to ruin a climax.

ABOUT THE AUTHOR

Regina Watts is the penname of a woman who certainly is not also M. F. Sullivan, founder and flagship author of Painted Blind Publishing. From her cozy home a few universes away from this one, Watts transmits stories to Sullivan that are then transcribed and published. Her available titles range from transgressive erotica to psychedelic fiction to horror to romance. Be sure to sign up for her mailing list at hrhdegenetrix.com!

ABOUT THE PUBLISHER

Painted Blind Publishing and its erotic imprint, Painted Blue Publishing, are the brainchild of author and devoted editor to Regina Watts, M. F. Sullivan. Founded in 2015 while Sullivan resided in Tucson, PBP is a house dedicated to bringing readers the finest in consciousness-expanding fiction. Be sure to check out the wide variety of essays available for free at paintedblindpublishing.com to learn more about the company, Watts, and Sullivan.

OTHER PAPERBACK WORKS
FROM PAINTED BLIND PUBLISHING

REGINA WATTS

INDUSTRIAL DIVINITY (2020)

WILD GIRL RUNNING (2020)

DOTTIE FOR YOU SEASON 1 (2021)

THE BURNINGSOUL SAGA (2021)

BE MY BULLY (2021)

SEDUCED BY SABINE (TBD)

M. F. SULLIVAN

DELILAH, MY WOMAN (2015)

THE LIGHTNING STENOGRAPHY DEVICE (2017)

THE DISGRACED MARTYR TRILOGY (2019-2020)